The first bullet ripped into the seat by her shoulder.

Bailey hunched over as the second cracked the windshield. Frank didn't wait for the third. He gunned the engine, pulling an evasive maneuver down a side street, and heard their tail screech in protest.

"Stay down!" Suddenly the black sedan swung behind them at the same time Frank noticed a semi ahead. He drove around the truck, using it as a shield and giving them the seconds they needed to get away.

After a couple of miles, he pulled over and helped her up. "Are you okay?" When she nodded, he said, "I'm taking you home now."

"No!" she said, sitting up suddenly. "I've come this far. I can't give up."

"Bailey, someone knows we're investigating this case and is trying to stop us. It probably goes way beyond that one man that was shooting at our car."

"Don't you realize one of those men already succeeded in killing my father?"

"And now they're trying to kill us."

Kathleen Tailer is a senior attorney II who works for the Supreme Court of Florida in the office of the state courts administrator. She graduated from Florida State University College of Law after earning her BA from the University of New Mexico. She and her husband have eight children, five of whom they adopted from the state of Florida. She enjoys photography and playing drums on the worship team at Calvary Chapel, Thomasville, Georgia.

Books by Kathleen Tailer

Love Inspired Suspense

Under the Marshal's Protection
The Reluctant Witness
Perilous Refuge
Quest for Justice

QUEST FOR JUSTICE

KATHLEEN TAILER

HARLEQUIN® LOVE INSPIRED® SUSPENSE

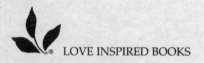 LOVE INSPIRED BOOKS

Recycling programs
for this product may
not exist in your area.

ISBN-13: 978-0-373-45726-7

Quest for Justice

Copyright © 2017 by Kathleen Tailer

www.Harlequin.com

Printed in U.S.A.

But those who hope in the Lord will renew their strength.
They will soar on wings like eagles; they will run and
not grow weary, they will walk and not be faint.
—Isaiah 40:31

For my wonderful husband, Jim,
and my amazing children: Bethany, Keandra,
Jessica, Nathan, Anna, Megan, Joshua and James.
It has been my honor to watch you grow into such fine,
courageous adults. I'm delighted to see how God is
using you each and every day to make the world
a better place. God has truly blessed me!

ONE

Bailey Cox eased carefully up to the corner of the building, her 9 mm Glock locked and loaded, but pointed at the darkened sky above her. Her finger tensed near the trigger as she moved slowly along the wall, sticking to the shadows. Her heart slammed wildly against her chest. She heard movement up ahead and voices, but they were muffled and she couldn't recognize them, or hear what they were saying. All she could tell was that they were angry. She moved closer, still not sure what to make of the situation. Her father, a private investigator, had texted her half an hour ago, asking her to rush over to his office because he'd had a break in the case he was working on and he needed her help.

Even though it was after 2:00 a.m., she hadn't hesitated and had headed out the door as soon as she had received her father's message. Bailey was used to staying up late and actually did her best thinking in the wee hours of the morning. She hadn't expected trouble but was now glad that she always traveled with her pistol.

When she'd arrived at her father's office, she'd found

the door cracked open and the small office abandoned. The light had still been on, and her father's coffee was still steaming on his desk, so he had to be nearby. It wasn't like him to call her and then not be there when she arrived. A tingle of fear shot down her spine. She'd heard noises in the alley behind her father's office building and had followed them, having no other clues to lead her.

The voices got louder. She eased around another corner and could barely make out two men arguing near a dark sedan parked by the Dumpster. The trunk door was open, and the men were gesturing toward its contents with angry waves. To her disappointment, neither man was her father. Still, she was glued to the argument as it played out in front of her. One of the men, dressed in a dark sweatshirt, moved closer to the car and kicked angrily at the bumper. They weren't arguing in a language she understood, which ruled out English, Spanish and French. If anything, she guessed it sounded Slavic, but she was no expert. A soft light emanated from a nearby street lamp, but it wasn't giving off enough light to help her identify either of the two men. Both had pale skin. The one in the sweatshirt had dark bushy hair. The other was in jeans and a black T-shirt and had dirty blond hair. Both were muscular and well built. The blond's face was red and seemed to darken with each passing minute as his anger consumed him. She edged closer.

"Freeze, or the next step you take will be your last." The words were whispered but as hard as steel. Bailey felt the cold metal barrel of the pistol against her neck and did as ordered. She hadn't heard anyone behind her and was instantly angry at herself for letting someone sneak up on her like that. She had been so focused on the men's argument that she had totally failed to watch her six. She tried to turn to see who was holding a gun on her, but as she did so, the gun pushed harder against her skin. She prayed the aggressor wasn't a friend of the two Slavic men.

"I said *freeze*. That doesn't mean move. Got it?" The deep voice was masculine and as cold as ice, but it also sounded familiar. Did she know this man? Her mind reeled. Even though he had spoken softly, a seed of dread was planted in her chest and she suddenly felt short of breath.

It couldn't be. Not here. Not now.

She almost wanted her assailant to speak again so she could prove herself mistaken. It couldn't be him. There was only one man on the planet who hated her and always thought the worst of her—Franklin Kennedy. She hadn't seen or heard from Kennedy in years, but she was certain Kennedy was still a cop. He was the kind of man who was born to work in law enforcement and would toe the line until he either got killed in the line of duty or retired to work in some security firm. He was a cop, through and through. He was also a straight arrow that never bent, regardless of the circumstances. But why would Kennedy be here at her father's office at two in the morning?

"Hands up. Slowly."

The voice was gritty, but still spoken so softly that she couldn't verify that it was Kennedy. The gun twisted slightly against her skin and she tensed, then she slowly raised her hands. The man reached forward and took her Glock and stowed it, then roughly shoved her up against the brick wall and frisked her, removing the small knife she had hidden in her waistband and the second pistol she'd secured in her ankle holster. He moved in closer so only she could hear his voice. She could even feel his exhalations warm against her neck and smell the mint from his breath. "Got any more hardware I should know about?"

"No," she answered softly, unable to keep the frustration out of her voice. "Look, I'm not trying to make trouble. My father called and when I got here, he wasn't in his office…" She tried to turn around to explain herself face-to-face, but he stopped her before she could turn, grabbed her wrists with one hand and cuffed her with the other.

"We got a report that there was a disturbance in this alley. The caller heard a gunshot, and you've got a gun. You have the right to remain silent. I suggest you exercise that right until we get this sorted out." He tightened the manacles until they bit into her skin. It was Kennedy. She was sure of it now. She didn't know how or why, but Franklin Kennedy now had her cuffed for the second time in her life. The first had been a living nightmare. She hoped this time wouldn't be a repeat. She pulled against the cuffs as frustration filled her.

"Easy." His voice was still low, and when he paused, she imagined he was listening to other policemen through an earpiece. When he spoke again, he wasn't talking to her and her suspicions were confirmed.

"Roger that. I've got one suspect in cuffs. You're a go. Repeat, you're a go."

Suddenly she heard screeching tires and blue police lights lit up the side of the building. The yelling around the corner escalated, but now it wasn't the foreign language she heard, but cops yelling at the two suspects to halt and put their hands up. The men didn't obey though, and she heard running and more shouting, but thankfully it sounded like they were moving away from her instead of getting closer. A few seconds later, gunfire erupted. Kennedy instantly pushed her to the ground, shielding her with his body, his own gun drawn, ready to shoot if they were threatened. For the first time, she got a glimpse of his face.

Clean-cut. Bold, direct features. It was Franklin Kennedy, alright. A spike of adrenaline soared through her veins.

"Stay low. Got it?" he growled.

He didn't wait for an answer and kept his eyes peeled on the area around them.

Bailey's fear erupted. What was going on? First her father had sent her that bizarre text, and the next thing she knew she was handcuffed by her nemesis just a block or so away from a gun battle. Was her father caught in the middle? Was he even involved at all? Questions filled her mind, as well as a sense of dread. None of this could be good. Being handcuffed and forced to give up her weapons hadn't helped matters. How was she going to help her father if she was under arrest?

The bullets stopped flying and she felt Kennedy relax

against her. He stood and pulled her to her feet. It was only then that he took a good look at his prisoner's face. His eyes widened and then narrowed.

"Bailey Cox?"

"In the flesh," she said with a touch of sass and then instantly regretted her tone. The last thing she needed to do was antagonize Kennedy while she was handcuffed and once again at his mercy.

He shifted, started to say something, apparently thought better of it and shook his head. Finally, he muttered, "I never thought I'd see you again."

"Same here," Bailey agreed.

"How long has it been? Five years?"

"Six." She said under her breath, "Six very long years."

He ignored her comment and a wave of anger seemed to sweep over him. "What are you doing armed to the teeth out here in the middle of the night?"

"My father is a private investigator and his office is in this building. He sent me a text and asked me to come over, so here I am. And I don't go anywhere unarmed."

Kennedy raised an eyebrow.

"Don't worry. I have a permit for the guns. It's in my wallet."

He raised his eyebrow and she continued. "I petitioned the court and got my rights reinstated. I'm allowed to carry a weapon." She swallowed. She would rather do anything else than ask for his help, but, at this point, she didn't have a choice.

"Look, I'm worried about my dad. His office was empty when I arrived, and I don't know what happened to him. I heard noise in the alley and came to investigate. That's it. I don't know anything about a gunshot, but I have to find my father and figure this out. Can you uncuff me?"

"No way." He grabbed her arm near the elbow and started leading her away from the building. "The firefight is over, but you're sitting on the sidelines until I get some answers. I don't want you in the middle of this."

She tried, but she couldn't keep the anxiety out of her voice. "You can't hold me. I haven't done anything wrong!"

"We'll see about that." His tone was icy. He led her toward the road where a nondescript sedan was parked against the curb.

A wave of desperation swept over her. "You can't do this. My father might be in danger. I have to find him…" She started to struggle but he held her firmly.

"What you have to do is settle down and let us get this scene secured." He pulled her roughly to the side of the car, apparently unaffected by her pleas or protests. One of her kicks caught him in the shin and he grimaced, but the next thing she knew, he had put his hand on her head, forced her into the back seat, closed the door and locked it. "Stay put and relax. I'll keep an eye out for your father while I'm working the scene."

His promise meant little to her. She wanted to be the one out there looking for him. She had a strong sense that something was terribly wrong and her father was either hurt or in grave danger, but with her hands cuffed and the door locked, there wasn't much she could do. Kennedy walked slowly away and then motioned to a uniformed officer who had just arrived on the scene and directed him to the car. "Stay with her. Watch her carefully. Don't let her escape or hurt herself. She's a person of interest. Got it?"

"Yes, sir." The officer nodded and took up his post outside her door.

"Kennedy!" she yelled futilely. "Come back here! I need to know what's going on!"

Franklin Kennedy ignored Bailey's pleas and headed over to the crime scene. He had heard most of what had happened on his earpiece, but he needed to check things out for himself. His fists clenched and unclenched as he approached. Bailey Cox! She was the last person he'd ever expected to see, although the fact that he'd found her in the middle of a crime scene was very telling. Six years ago, Bailey Cox had been his first arrest after he'd made detective with the Jacksonville sheriff's office.

She'd only been twenty years old then, but her youth and inexperience hadn't stopped her from stealing over a million dollars from a large real estate firm's escrow account. Bailey Cox was an incredible hacker and had somehow managed to move the money right under the noses of the firm's security team. The money had never been recovered. She'd been busted on some other smaller charges and had served some time, but Bailey's case was the one that bothered him the most since he'd joined the force. She had basically gotten away with her crimes, and, in his book, that was just plain wrong. And where was the stolen money?

A knot formed in the pit of his stomach. He'd had a

soft spot for Bailey Cox before she'd stolen that money. He'd run into her several times when he'd been a beat cop, newly on the job, and she was a brash teenager. In fact, he'd even felt sorry for her back then. She'd had a tough start and gotten in with a bad crowd on more than one occasion. Her mother was a meth user who valued drugs above her daughter's welfare, and her father had abandoned them both years before. She'd basically been left to her own devices, and although she was smart, she'd still made a series of horrible choices.

She'd always had a smile on her face, however, and been full of fire. She was one of those who was given lemons and somehow always figured out how to make lemonade. He admired that.

Once she'd moved up to committing felonies, however, his soft spot had hardened. Now when he thought of Bailey Cox, he felt nothing but anger and frustration. Sure, she'd had a rough life, but nothing justified her crimes. Still, when she looked at him with those dark blue eyes of hers, it still affected him, even though he fought the feelings.

He pushed the thoughts of Bailey aside and approached the scene where gunfire had erupted. A dark-haired man wearing a sweatshirt was lying faceup in a pool of blood. He certainly wouldn't be answering any questions, but hopefully they could get other clues from the scene. Already two uniformed officers were putting up police tape while another was bagging and tagging the offender's gun. He had obviously been firing on the officers when he'd been shot.

"Hey, Frankie." Another detective from his unit, Ben Graham, was leaning near the body and nodded at him.

Frank returned the nod. "What have you got?"

"Here's the first one. The other is around the corner. Both were firing on us, and both are now dead, shot by our team. We didn't have much choice." Ben stood and motioned down the alley. "Take a walk over to the vehicle by the Dumpster and look in the trunk."

Frank rose an eyebrow and walked over to where the car still sat with the trunk door open. There wasn't much light from the street lamp, so he pulled out his flashlight and shone it in the trunk of the car.

There was quite a bit of blood pooled around the body, especially around the man's gunshot wound in the forehead. He turned to the cop who was standing by the car. "You got a name for our victim?"

"Yeah. His wallet had a photo ID. You're looking at Matt Cox."

Frank leaned closer to get a better look, not wanting to believe what he was seeing. Bailey's father's dead eyes stared back at him.

TWO

Franklin Kennedy stepped up to the table where Bailey Cox was manacled in the interrogation room and took a seat across from her. She'd been there for over three hours while they had verified her story, and so far everything she'd said had checked out. They'd found the text on her cell phone, and she did indeed have a concealed weapons permit, despite her criminal history.

She'd been in the wrong place at the wrong time just because she was worried about her father—and now he had to tell her she'd never see the man again.

Frank hated giving death notices. He dropped the file on the table and leaned back. She was antsy and her hands moved constantly, giving away just how uncomfortable she was in the police station. He said nothing for several minutes, and his quiet seemed to unnerve her.

Finally, she gave a frustrated groan. "Well? Are you ready to release me? I've been here for hours."

"Not quite yet, Ms. Cox."

"You've known me half of my life. You might as well call me Bailey." She leaned back. "Surely you've had time to check my cell phone and verify my story."

Frank nodded. "We have. We found the text."

Bailey's eyes widened. "So? What else are you waiting for? I've got to go find my father. You can't just hold me here forever. I haven't done anything wrong."

Frank shrugged and eyed her closely. She hadn't changed much in the last six years. Her face was more mature and she'd grown into her figure, but her eyes held the quick intelligence they always had, and her high cheekbones and full lips still made her one of the most attractive women he'd ever seen. In his book, it was a pity that such beauty was wasted on a criminal.

She spoke again and her voice was caustic. "You've heard of false imprisonment, right? I mean, they do teach you *something* at the police academy."

He ignored her comment. She'd always had a feisty mouth. Her refusal to be cowed was actually something he admired about her. Even when the chips were down, she was a firecracker, vivacious and spirited.

Finally, he opened the folder and sifted through the papers it contained that detailed her life for the last six years. After prison, she'd worked in Mobile, Alabama, taking night classes in computer science until she got her degree. She lived a simple lifestyle. No extravagant purchases. What had happened to the money she stole? Was she afraid that if she spent it, he would be able to trace it back to her? His mind was full of questions, but he held his tongue. Now wasn't the right time, especially because he saw the vulnerability shining in her eyes beneath that tough veneer.

Deep down, he knew he was focusing on the money because he didn't want to think about the conversation they needed to have. Somehow, he had to figure out how to tell her about her father's death. He raked his fingers through his shortly cropped hair, unable to avoid the task any longer. "We found your father."

She sat up quickly. "Where? Is he okay?"

He leaned forward, unlocked the handcuffs and then pocketed them. She rubbed her wrists and stood. "So?" Her face was expectant and so full of life and vibrancy that he hated to say the next words.

"I'm sorry to tell you that your father has been killed, Bailey."

Bailey slowly sat back down. Her eyes widened and he saw a flicker of pain before her face became a mask. "How? Where?"

"We found him with a fatal gunshot wound. He was in the back of that sedan that was parked behind his office building. The two men who probably committed the crime are also dead after they fired upon police officers. We're running forensic tests right now to verify that one of their guns was the weapon used to shoot him."

"Why was he killed?"

"We don't know yet. We're investigating that now."

"No! You're lying!" She lunged at him across the table and he grabbed her hands, stopping the onslaught.

"He can't be dead!" She was really upset now. Maybe he should have waited to release her from the handcuffs, but he couldn't imagine telling her that kind of news with her hands manacled. Still, she was clearly out of control. For the second time today, he found himself bearing the brunt of her temper. She struggled against him, but he was much stronger and easily overpowered her. He pulled her to the side of the table and into a tight hold with her back against his chest and her arms secured so she could do no further damage. Sobs racked her body. She finally gave up her struggles and just sagged against him, the tears pouring down her face.

Her pain touched him. Sure, she was a criminal and justice had never been served in her case, but she was clearly suffering. He wouldn't wish this type of agony on his worst enemy. He held her tightly, letting his strength buoy her up. He would hold her for as long as she needed. It was the least he could do, despite her past and his feelings about it.

Bailey just couldn't hold it in. He couldn't be dead. Her grief was overwhelming. Although her father had abandoned her as a child, Bailey had finally been able to forgive him and move forward with their relationship within the past year. It had been a slow and bumpy process, but getting to know her father had been a big part of her life over the last few months. She had even started working with him on his cases, and they were becoming a formidable team. How could all of that be over?

Once her tears ebbed, she felt numb and listless but savored the feel of warmth and security that Franklin Kennedy offered in his embrace. He might be her enemy, but at least now she knew he was human. He was aware of her criminal history and everything she had done, yet he still didn't push her away in her hour of need. She was grateful and also a bit surprised.

Finally, she caught her breath and stepped back from his touch. He offered her a handkerchief and she took

it and wiped her eyes. Who carried handkerchiefs anymore? It was an inane thought, but it distracted her for a
moment, and she wanted desperately to think about anything but her father's final fate. She took another step
back, embarrassed by her behavior. "I'm sorry. I guess
I feel overwhelmed by all of this, but I didn't mean to
take it out on you. Please forgive me." She softened her
voice as she brushed some stray hairs away from her
face. "So where is his body?"

"At the morgue. I need to take you over there to identify him when you're ready."

"Is that why you kept me here so long?"

Kennedy nodded. "It's one of the reasons. I didn't
want you to see him in the trunk of that car. That
shouldn't be your last memory of him. By the time we
get downtown, they'll have him cleaned up a bit." He
paused. "I'm sorry, Bailey. I really am."

She nodded and was silent for a moment, trying to
gather her thoughts. Okay. Kennedy had scored two
points today in the humane category. They could never
be friends, but at least some of her anger toward him
had dwindled. Maybe he didn't hate her after all. Six
years ago, Kennedy had pursued her relentlessly and
had finally caught her red-handed with the stolen medical equipment that her mother needed to survive. She'd
been convicted and sentenced, but, even so, she doubted
he counted it as a victory.

They both knew the prosecutor had failed to gather
enough evidence to convict her of her more serious
crime—stealing a little over a million dollars to pay
for her mother's medical bills. However, her mother

had died shortly after the theft, and Bailey had actually spent very little of it. It was currently hidden away in an offshore account, well concealed from local law enforcement and the forensic accountants they'd hired.

She pushed those thoughts aside and focused on the here and now. A new thought hit her. "So who were the two men behind my father's building?"

Kennedy shrugged. "I'm not at liberty to say."

She narrowed her eyes. "You're kidding, right? I think I have a right to know who killed my father."

He pursed his lips, apparently unwilling to answer her.

She pressed on. "Were they American?"

He still didn't answer.

"Oh, come on, Kennedy. You won't be giving away government secrets by letting me know what my father stumbled into."

"That's Detective Kennedy, Bailey, and I meant it when I said I'm not at liberty to say. There's an ongoing investigation in place. That's really all you need to know."

She fumed inwardly but could tell that he wasn't going to budge. At least not today. She let the issue drop for now but resolved to revisit it once things settled down. She was going to find out why her father had been killed. That was the bottom line.

It was time to go. She needed to get the viewing over with and then hide away in her apartment so she could just be alone in her pain. "Let's do this," she said quietly, trying to mask her grief. They left the interrogation room and she gathered her phone and keys from the desk sergeant as they left the station. She didn't protest when Kennedy held on to her guns and knife, knowing her objection would be futile. She wasn't actually surprised at his precaution since he had seen her temper flare so much today. Probably the last thing he wanted was for her to lose it again and have her gun in her hand at the same time.

He always seemed to catch her at her worst. Even though she'd made admirable attempts to turn her life around, Kennedy would always see her as a criminal.

They arrived at the morgue and were greeted by a worker who took them to a small room with a window covered by thick, dark curtains. Kennedy met her eye. "Are you ready?"

"As ready as I can be," Bailey answered. "Go ahead."

Kennedy pushed the button on the intercom near the window. "We're ready."

The curtain opened and showed a medical room behind the glass. She gasped as the attendant pulled back the sheet. The body was definitely her father, but she hadn't been prepared for the damage the bullet had caused. It was a horrible image that she was afraid was going to stay with her for several years to come. She nodded and the attendant quickly put the sheet back over the body. She gripped the handkerchief, praying she wouldn't start bawling right here at the morgue.

"I'll take you home," Kennedy said softly.

She glanced up at him and their eyes connected. There was compassion there, yet still the determination and grit that she had always seen in him since he had first snapped the cuffs around her wrists six years ago.

But, in this case, his determination was a good thing. If he was assigned to solve her father's murder, then he wouldn't give up until he had the culprit behind bars.

"Are you going to be working this case?"

"I am," he confirmed.

A wave of satisfaction swept over her. "So am I," she said vehemently. "One of those two goons in the alley probably pulled the trigger, but there has to be more to this. I'm going to find out who and why and make them pay."

He put his hands up. "No, you're not. You're going to go home and stay out of the way while I do my job. I don't need or want your help."

"That's not the way it works, Detective," she said grimly. "He was my father. I'm going to get to the bottom of this, no matter what it takes."

THREE

Bailey opened the office door, then bent under the crime scene tape and closed the door quickly behind her. She ignored the light switch and instead flipped on her small flashlight, seeking out her father's desk. After her long night at the police station and the morgue, she'd tried to sleep at her apartment but hadn't been able to keep her mind off her father's murder. Once night had fallen again, she'd decided to start her investigation, which meant going back to her father's office and looking for clues.

She continued her perusal of the desktop and noted that her father's laptop was missing, but she didn't know if the police had taken it as part of their investigation or if someone else had acted. It didn't actually matter either way. Her father was a Luddite, tried and true, and kept meticulous paper files for every case. She looked around her father's desktop for any notes or hints regarding the case he'd been working on when he'd texted her, but she found nothing. Either the notes had also been taken or he hadn't written anything down.

Maybe she was missing something obvious—she

couldn't know for sure. She wasn't the experienced investigator her father was. But Bailey's computer skills were unparalleled, and she had been able to help her father close several cases during her short tenure by finding old emails and other items that the perpetrator had thought he'd deleted, or by tracking down trails on the internet that led to the party's guilt. The internet was a gold mine of information if a person knew where to look. Nothing was ever really erased. Thankfully, she was a really good miner.

Thankfully. She thought about that word for a moment. Despite everything that was happening in her life, she always tried to recognize and appreciate the good things going on around her. Even with her father's death shadowing her, she was still thankful that she was alive and both willing and able to pursue the case so the murderer would be brought to justice. She also had her health, a small savings account and she shouldn't have any trouble finding another job once this investigation was over. That was a lot to be thankful for.

She made her way over to the filing cabinet, unlocked it and pulled out the first few files that were classified as Pending. The first file was a simple divorce and didn't seem to have any unique issues, but the second caught her interest and she poured over the pages, lost in concentration.

She didn't hear the man enter behind her, and when she finally did sense his presence, it was too late. The blow to her head caught her near her right ear, and she instantly saw black and passed out as her body slumped to the floor.

* * *

Franklin Kennedy eased his car around the corner, and then he slowed and stopped completely. What was going on in Cox's office? He'd been driving by and had seen a light flicker in the window. He waited. There it was again. The yellow police tape was still blocking the door and the overhead lights were off, but he could see a flashlight moving behind the window. He parked and pulled out his own flashlight, as well as his service revolver. There shouldn't be anyone in that office—especially with the crime tape still blocking the doorway. He approached the front door but noticed that the light inside had disappeared. He tried the door, but it was locked. He shone the light in the window but couldn't see any movement or other signs of life. What had happened to the light he'd seen? He edged around the building, keeping his gun and flashlight pointed ahead of him, not sure what to expect.

Suddenly he heard footsteps, but they were running away from him. He felt his adrenaline spike and he moved faster toward the back of the building. He arrived around the corner just in time to hear tires squeal away. The flashlight illuminated a dark sedan, but it was too dark to make out the plate or even the make and model of the car. He moved cautiously to the back door of the building and tried the knob. The door opened in his hand.

He was fairly certain that he had scared off whoever had been in the office suite, but he needed to investigate nonetheless. The forensic team had already come and gone, but had law enforcement missed something?

What was so important that someone felt the need to break in? The crime tapes usually stayed up until after all of the interviews were completed, just in case they had to return and look for more evidence as a result of new information gained through the interview process. So far his interviews had yielded zilch, which almost guaranteed he would be returning at some point, just in case he could discover a new clue. He turned on the light switch by the back door and stowed his flashlight.

The groan surprised him, and he instantly raised his gun. "Sheriff's department. Show yourself. Now."

No one answered and he advanced slowly, not sure what to expect. He stepped around an overturned table and a mess on the floor and then he spotted Bailey Cox, lying prone on the floor. He glanced around to make sure there wasn't someone hiding in the shadows. Seeing no one, he holstered his gun and rushed to her side.

"Bailey? Are you okay?"

Bailey slowly opened her eyes and winced. Her hand went instantly to her wound. Franklin caught her hand and gently moved it away so he could get a better look at her injury.

"Kennedy?"

"Yeah, it's me. What are you doing in here? It was blocked off for a reason." It was too soon for her to be in here. Any evidence they seized now would be tainted. He pushed the regulations out of his head and focused on Bailey. She obviously hadn't been the only one here. Someone else thought there was something to find in this office as well and was trying to make sure Bailey and the police remained clueless. What had they missed?

Bailey squinted against the light and moaned again. There was a large bump forming over her right ear and a trickle of blood matted her hair. That seemed to be her only injury. He stood and looked around for a freezer containing some ice, but the office didn't have one, so he headed to the bathroom and then returned with a cool, wet hand towel. As he returned, Bailey was trying to sit up, but he gently pushed her back down.

"Here, take this. It might help," he said softly as he put the towel in her hand.

She pushed the towel away, suddenly agitated. "The files…where are they?"

"You're bleeding." He took the towel back and started carefully cleaning her wound. He was surprised that she allowed his ministrations, but her docility was probably due to the pain. A wound like that had to hurt. "Is that better?"

"Yes. Thank you." She took a deep breath. "You wouldn't happen to have any aspirin, would you?"

"Not on me. Sorry. Did your dad keep any here in the office?"

"I don't remember seeing any," she said softly.

"Did you see who hit you?"

"No, I was reading a file…" She suddenly tried to sit up again and her eyes darted quickly around her. This time, he helped her up to a sitting position. She kept the towel pressed against her wound as she looked around. Her shoulders slumped. "The files are gone."

"What files?"

"My dad kept hard copies of his files that mirrored the files on his computer, but the written versions went into a lot more detail. I was reading through the files for his open investigations when someone came in here and hit me. I only got a chance to look at a couple of them. Whoever hit me must have taken the files when they left. I had a whole stack of them sitting right here." She motioned toward an empty spot on the floor.

"Well, it's a good thing I interrupted him when I did. If I hadn't, he might have killed you."

Bailey shrugged. "Even so, I'm not going to stop investigating. I told you I'm going to find out who ordered my father's murder. That's exactly what I intend to do, with or without those files."

"And I told you to stay away from this case. You're too close." He leaned back. "We took his computer as part of our investigation and have a team of experts going over it as we speak."

"That's not going to do you much good. He barely used the thing."

Kennedy shrugged. "Even so…"

"Aren't you the one investigating? Shouldn't you be the one going over it?" Her voice was skeptical, and her tone bothered him, although he wasn't sure why. Why should he care what she thought of him? He pushed the thought away and focused on the conversation. Maybe he could learn something valuable from Bailey. Sometimes witnesses and family members knew things that they didn't even realize would help solve the case. He wanted her to relax her guard around him. She just might let something important slip.

"Yes, I went through his computer earlier today, but I didn't see anything that would raise a red flag. I'm not a hacker, though. I needed a bit of help, and police work is a team effort."

She raised an eyebrow. "And what have you and your squad discovered?"

Protocol meant he shouldn't answer her—but if he wanted her to open up to him, he'd have to give a little. "Nothing yet. Everything so far seems rather routine. Nothing worth killing over, at any rate. He hadn't even updated any of his computer files for over two weeks. Whatever he discovered the night he was killed isn't noted on the hard drive. We'll keep going over it, though, as the case progresses. Once we have a few leads, we might see something that ties everything together."

"That's why you need me. I might see something that you and your team don't. I can save you valuable time."

Frank shook his head. There was no way he was working with a convicted felon on a murder investigation, especially when the victim was the felon's father. It was a recipe for disaster. Still, he hadn't interviewed her yet regarding the murder, so now was as good a time as any. He'd planned on looking her up tomorrow anyway. "Look, you were working with your dad, right? How well did you know the cases he was working on?"

She paused for a moment, displeased that he had changed the subject, before apparently deciding to let him get away with it. "We've only been working together for the last six months or so. I don't know all of his cases. I only worked with him on those that required computer expertise. That's why I came here today—to learn more about the other ones that I wasn't working on, but now that the files are missing, I'll need to see his computer to get the names and details of the other clients."

Frank ignored her subtle push to access her father's computer and sat on the corner of her father's desk. "So, how many cases were you working?"

"Bits and pieces of four of them."

"Do you see any connections between those cases and his death?"

"No. Like you said before, nothing worth killing over. Three of the cases are common divorces with the parties trying to hide assets, but none of them are worth more than about 150K. The other is a young lady that was adopted as an infant who is looking for her birth parents. I've already made a lot of progress on that case—I've found the birth mother and have leads on the biological father. Everyone involved seems pretty ordinary, so I doubt that has anything to do with my father's death, either."

"Did your dad have a backup hard drive?"

Bailey shook her head. "No. I was trying to get him to back up his laptop, but he kept telling me that's what the paper files were for." She pulled herself to her feet, swayed a bit and grabbed the wall for support.

Frank stood and quickly led her to her father's office chair and had her sit again. Rather than appreciating his help, however, she pulled her arm roughly away from him.

"I'm okay."

He put up his hands in mock surrender. "Maybe you should take it easy for a while. I can call an ambulance if you need one."

"Don't you dare," she said in a low voice. "I'm perfectly fine."

"Sure you are." He returned to sitting on the side of the desk. He wasn't going to argue with her, but he was going to make sure she was okay and could safely get home before he left her this evening.

"So when can I get my father's computer back?"

"It's going to be a while."

"Look, let's just cut through the dancing. Since the files were stolen, I need that computer to find out what case is related to his murder. Even if it hasn't been updated, I might be able to make a connection."

"That's not going to happen." He could see the anger erupting within her, but to her credit, she didn't lash out this time. He tried to mollify her. "Look. We're both making a very big assumption here—that his death is related to one of his cases."

"He led a pretty simple life. I can't imagine he was into anything dangerous outside of his work." She paused.

He drew his lips into a thin line.

Bailey visibly fumed but still managed to hold her temper. He ran his hand through his hair and decided to change the subject again. "Let's take a step back. Did your dad have any enemies?"

Bailey exhaled. "Not that I know of, but to be fair, I've only been working with him for the last six months or so, and he didn't share everything with me. Before we started working together, I didn't even know him that well, but I still can't imagine that he was into anything dangerous."

Franklin thought about that for a minute. From what he remembered, Bailey's parents had divorced when she was a baby, and while her mother had used drugs and neglected her, leaving her on her own to raise herself, the story went that her father had basically abandoned her. "I thought you didn't get along with your father."

"I didn't even know him, but after I got out of prison, I looked him up and found out the truth. My parents got married right after my father joined the military. He was sent overseas, and my mom got lonely and started self-medicating with drugs and alcohol. She never even told him she was pregnant before they divorced. My father left the military and took a post in Germany where he worked for years. He never remarried." She took a breath. "He didn't even know I existed until I walked through his door."

Frank absorbed this information. He could tell it had taken a lot out of her to share such a painful story. He had also felt the sting of abandonment during his life and was glad that she had at least been able to reconcile with her father before his death. He paused for a few moments, lost in thought, then moved on. "What about his past cases? Any unhappy customers?"

Bailey shook her head. "Again, not that I know of." She met his eye when she spoke, but then he noticed her studying the items on her father's desk. The cup of coffee her father had been drinking before his death was still sitting on the coaster, now with a slight film on the top. There was some mail in a pile, including a few bills. They'd already checked out his accounts and discovered that Cox was up-to-date with his payments and his business was financially sound. His death wasn't tied to money troubles.

Franklin grimaced, remembering his disappointment at finding that Cox didn't have any unusually large amounts of cash in any of his accounts. He'd secretly hoped that Bailey had given him some of the money she'd stolen, which would give him an excuse to hunt for the stolen cash once again. Unfortunately, all he'd found were the normal debts and purchases of a man making the salary he'd claimed on his tax returns.

He watched Bailey carefully. Yes, she had already done her time, but it burned him that she had gotten off for stealing the money and only gotten a light two-year sentence for the other thefts. No one should benefit from breaking the law. But she'd had her day in court and she had won. They couldn't even prove she had the cash, and jeopardy had attached. She couldn't be tried twice for the same crime, even if they discovered new evidence. Deep down, he knew she had taken the money and he couldn't let her get away with it.

Before this case was over, he wanted more than just to find Cox's killer. He wanted Bailey Cox to lead him to the stolen money so he could close that case once and for all.

FOUR

Bailey crossed her legs right over left and a few seconds later moved them back to left over right. Her left hand nervously drummed a tune. Her dress slacks and shirt were the only formal clothes she owned, and she wore them so infrequently that they made her incredibly uncomfortable. She was a jeans-and-T-shirt kind of girl. But she would dress the part if needed to find out who murdered her father. She anxiously glanced around the room. How much longer would she have to wait? That was another thing she wasn't good at—waiting.

Thankfulness, she told herself. She needed to remember and focus on the good, not the bad. She was thankful that she had the appropriate clothing for this meeting and thankful that she had gotten a meeting with the VP of Gates Industries in the first place. There were always blessings all around her. All she had to do was take the time to look and notice them.

She looked around the posh waiting room and noticed a dark-haired man in black clothes sitting across from her, thumbing through a magazine. She couldn't put her finger on it, but something about him made her uncomfortable. He glanced at her and she gave him a smile, but he frowned and returned to his magazine, and the dislike she'd seen in his eyes made her skin start to crawl. She stood and paced a bit, avoiding the man and trying to release some of her nervous energy.

The police department still hadn't returned her father's computer, and since the paper files were missing, she was now following the only lead she had. Her father's coffee cup on his desk had been a fancy new mug emblazoned with the Gates Industries design. She had never seen that cup before, so she was hoping her father had gotten it when he'd taken on Gates as a new client. The lead was really weak, but it was all she had.

Bailey knew a bit about Gates—they were a large pharmaceutical company in both the American and the international markets. What her father could have been doing for them was anybody's guess, but she was hoping that there was a connection, however thin, that would give her some insight into that terrible night of her father's death. Gates's vice president had agreed to see her, but his last meeting was running late. She gave up the pacing and sat back down again and checked her watch.

"Sure is a surprise meeting you here."

She jumped at the voice and dread filled her. Franklin Kennedy sat down in the seat beside her, and she warily glanced his way.

"What are you doing here?"

He pursed his lips and then spoke. "I think the real question is, what are you doing here?"

She bristled. "I'm here investigating my father's death, just like I told you I would."

Kennedy's eyes narrowed. "And I told you to stay away from this. Do I have to arrest you to keep you out of the way?"

"Yeah, I guess you'd better because there's no way I'm sitting at home while you track down whoever caused his death. I need answers."

She saw his eyes grow cold at her defiance, but she meant what she'd said. She wasn't going to sit by and let others chase down his murderer when she was perfectly capable of investigating the crime.

She watched Kennedy carefully, ready to jump and run if she needed to. His eyes showed that he was considering his options and she watched his hands as well, waiting to see if he started to reach for his handcuffs. When he shifted, she jumped to her feet, and the tension in the room seemed palpable. She swallowed hard.

"Well?" she challenged.

"You haven't told me what you're doing here yet." He gave her a smile, but his demeanor was anything but friendly. Still, he stayed seated and didn't look like he was about to arrest her for obstruction. "Care to share?"

She considered this. She knew Franklin Kennedy was a good cop. It still irked her, however, that he expected her to share when he wasn't willing to let her help with the investigation. Hiding clues from him was foolhardy, though, especially when they were after the same thing—justice. "I saw a new mug from Gates on my father's desk. I'm guessing they hired him, and I'm here to find out why. It's not much of a lead, but it's all

I've got since the files are missing and I can't access my father's computer."

Kennedy studied her for a few moments and his scrutiny made her even more nervous. Finally, he seemed to come to a decision and leaned back in the chair.

"Smart deduction. Gates *is* one of his newest accounts, and it was the last file that was open on his computer before his death. We think he was about to update his notes when he was interrupted, so we wanted to check it out, as well. In this case, your instincts are pretty good."

She breathed a sigh of relief at his words. "So I can stay?"

Kennedy's pause made her nervousness return, but he finally nodded at her. "For now." He raised an eyebrow. "I'm going to join you for your appointment. But let me ask the questions, okay? Do you think you can do that?"

Could she? Keeping her mouth shut was not her forte, but if the choices were staying silent during the interview or occupying a jail cell, she'd definitely choose the former. She nodded and took her seat again, just as a secretary came to announce that the VP was ready to see her. Kennedy stood, introduced himself and explained that they needed to see the VP together. After seeing his badge, the secretary accepted his request and led them both past reception into the hallway. Bailey turned and looked over her shoulder one last time at the dark-haired man. Now he was watching her, and his eyes seemed to bore right through her as she walked. She didn't know the man, but his expression was so intense that she was glad to get away from him. If looks could kill, she'd be lying dead on the floor right now.

The secretary led them to Mr. Johnson's office, where a tall, graying man was seated behind a desk, working on a laptop. He closed the computer as they entered and rose before motioning toward the chairs in front of his desk.

They all shook hands before Frank spoke up. "Thank you for seeing us. I'm Detective Kennedy, and this is Bailey Cox. I had an appointment with you later today, but Ms. Cox and I thought we'd save you some time and talk to you together. We have a few questions we'd like to ask you."

"I'm happy to help in any way I can," Johnson said smoothly. They all sat and Kennedy opened up his iPad and started taking notes. "You've probably heard that Matt Cox was killed a couple of nights ago. We were hoping you could tell us about the work he was doing for you."

"Sure," Johnson said as he leaned back in his chair. "Gates Industries is headed for change. Our current CEO and president is stepping down at the end of the year, and we're in the process of vetting the applicants for the position. Mr. Cox was investigating the backgrounds of the five finalists. He was due to give us his full report at the end of the month."

Frank's fingers flew over his iPad screen, documenting Mr. Johnson's answer. "Had he told you anything he'd discovered yet?"

Johnson nodded. "He sent us a preliminary report

about two weeks ago. I scanned it but unfortunately didn't have time to read through the whole thing. As far as I know, though, nothing odd stood out on any of the applicants. Mr. Cox had completed the basic checks and was beginning to dig deeper. You know, interviewing references, that sort of thing." He shifted. "Do you really think that his murder is related to the work he was doing for Gates?"

Frank shrugged. "We're exploring every avenue at this point. Do you think we could get a copy of his initial report? We found one on his computer, but we want to make sure they match up."

"Of course," Johnson answered. "If you give my assistant your email address, I'll have her send it to you."

"That would be great. Did Mr. Cox have contact with anyone else here at Gates?"

Again, Johnson shook his head. "Not that I know of. I'm the one who hired him, and I had an appointment set to meet with him once he'd finished the job. Then I was going to present his report and findings to the board."

Frank glanced at Bailey, who looked like she was about to burst. He had to give her credit. She was doing a good job of keeping quiet and fulfilling her promise. He looked back at his notes. "Is it standard procedure to hire a private investigator to do background checks on your prospective employees?" he asked.

"I can't speak to other companies and their procedures, but it's standard for upper management positions here at Gates. You'd be surprised by how many people lie on their applications. I guess they figure that companies don't check, which is exactly why we do."

Frank wrote down a few more things and then looked up. "Sounds like a good policy. Would you mind giving me the names of the five candidates?"

"Not at all. In fact, I'd appreciate any information you gain from your investigation that might have a bearing on our hiring decision. With Mr. Cox gone, we'll have to hire a new investigator. That will really mess up our timeline."

"Will you have to forgo some of the background checks?"

Johnson looked uncomfortable. "The board hasn't decided. We might just go with Cox's preliminary findings."

"Does Gates have any enemies? Anybody who would like to see the leadership struggle?"

"Sure," Johnson answered. "Atlantic Medical Supply is probably our staunchest competitor. We're both bidding on a large contract with Nextco, a company that makes three of our biggest sellers."

"And what happens if Gates doesn't get the contract?"

"Well, we'll have to lay off about one hundred workers." He held up his hands. "I'm trusting you not to share that information. It's one of the reasons the board is in a hurry to fill the position. We need a strong leader to secure the contract."

"Do you have a frontrunner in this search?" Frank asked.

"We've been leaning toward Gabriel Jeffries, an entrepreneur who has done amazing things in the market. If the decision had to be made today, he would probably be the one selected, unless we discover some horrible skeleton in his closet. He has the most experience and would take our company in the right direction." Johnson stood and motioned toward the door. "I'll walk you out and get my assistant to send you that list of applicants and Mr. Cox's preliminary report."

They all walked back out to the secretary's desk and she quickly emailed both of the promised items to Frank's work email address. He noticed Bailey looking around the reception area as if expecting to see someone, but the room was empty. To his surprise, she stayed quiet until they had left the Gates building and were standing on the sidewalk.

"Okay," she said, her eyebrows raised. "I held up my end and didn't ask a single question. Can you share the list of applicants and report with me?"

Frank shook his head. "Our deal was that I let you in on the interview instead of arresting you. I didn't say anything about sharing the list. We still don't even know if this case has anything to do with your father's murder, but, either way, that's for me to investigate. You need to go home now and let me do my job."

Her face flushed with anger. "Hold on now. I thought we were working together on this."

Frank laughed. "I don't know what gave you that idea. I certainly never said that."

His response only seemed to make her angrier. "You implied it. I have a lot to offer."

"I'll give you a *million* reasons why that will never work."

She raised an eyebrow. "So we're singing that old song again, are we?"

"And we'll keep singing it until you return the money." Frank leaned forward. She was so close that he could feel her breath on his skin. When he spoke, his voice was low but forceful, and his words were for her ears alone. "You never served a day in prison for stealing all of that money. Do you honestly think that's right?"

Bailey narrowed her eyes. "I was acquitted, remember? The DA tried to pin it on me and failed. The medical equipment was all anyone could prove I had stolen, and I served my time for that."

"That stolen equipment was just the tip of the iceberg," Frank said, his voice still deceptively soft. "You know it and I know it. You might have beaten the court system, but I still want the money you stole returned, and I'm not going to stop pushing until we get it all back. Every last cent. When you're ready to turn it over, come see me. Otherwise, stay out of my way."

She grimaced. "I need that list and my father's report. I'll trade you for them—do some computer work for you or…"

Frank leaned back. "We're done here. Go home, Bailey."

She put her hands on her hips. "I won't," she said stubbornly.

He moved closer again and she took a step back. "Tell me where the money is, Bailey. It's the right thing to do." She met his eyes but said nothing.

Frank stepped away. "Good-bye, Bailey."

FIVE

Frank turned on his heel and walked away, leaving her standing in front of Gates. He definitely needed to get as far away from Bailey Cox as possible before he was forced to admit that he found her attractive when she showed her strength and determination. He ran his hand through his hair in frustration, angry with himself and the jumble of emotions that were flying through him. Why couldn't he control his feelings? She was a criminal and an unrepentant one at that. Yet, without seeming to even realize it, she was drawing him closer like a moth to a flame, and his skin was already feeling the singe.

He widened his steps and sped up, suddenly in a hurry to get to his car and be off. It was ridiculous for him to feel anything for her besides contempt when she was still hiding the money she'd stolen. Sure, the case had gone cold years ago, and since the insurance company had paid the tab, nobody was really even looking for the money—except him. He just couldn't let it go, even though it was probably a fool's hope that he'd ever track it down.

He pushed his feelings aside and focused on the murder investigation. There was no reason to ever see her again, and that thought gave him some degree of satisfaction. For a moment, he'd thought he'd seen something in Bailey's eyes that made him believe she was willing to make a bargain, but he had been wrong. She wouldn't even talk about the money, and without that dialogue, he was done. It was time for them to go their separate ways.

He reached his car but couldn't shake a strange feeling that he was being watched. He scanned the area but didn't see Bailey or anybody else paying any attention to him. Still, hot electricity ran down his back. He checked again and this time noticed a man in black eyeing him from across the street. Frank pocketed his keys and headed across the street to confront the man, but several cars drove by and blocked him from crossing. By the time Frank reached the doorway where the man had been standing, there was no sign of him. Why had the man been watching him?

His stomach rumbled and he decided to stick around and grab a quick bite in case the man reappeared. He glanced up and down the street and then headed toward a nearby coffee shop and turned his thoughts back to Gates.

The company didn't look like much of a lead at this point, but he would follow through and check out the five applicants, just in case. It seemed ridiculous to kill over a career opportunity, but he'd actually seen worse as a beat cop. Maybe he was jaded, but few things surprised him anymore. In any case, the list of applicants from Gates was his best lead so far. Hopefully interviewing them would point him to the killer.

He placed his order at the counter and then called his office while he waited.

"Graham."

"Hey, this is Frank." He gave Ben Graham a synopsis of the discussion with Johnson, smiled at the waitress who handed him his food and headed for a table, his ear still pressed against the phone. "Anything new on the Cox case?"

Ben cleared his throat. "We've got a couple of new reports. Forensics matched the bullet to the gun in the blond man's possession. So now we know who pulled the trigger, but we still don't know his identity. According to our databases, he's a ghost. The dark-haired man we've positively identified as Adrian Bekim from Balkavia. He's an international gun for hire and did most of his work in Europe until recently, when he surfaced in Chicago. He's suspected in the death of a businessman there."

Frank soaked in the information. "Still nothing from CODIS on the blond?" he asked, referring to the national DNA index system.

"Not yet. Nothing from the national fingerprint and criminal history system, either."

Frank grimaced. "I'm thinking it's time to contact Interpol. The blond is probably a known associate of Bekim. He's got to show up somewhere."

"Yep, I'll start the process." Ben paused. "You should also know that we've finished examining Cox's financials. There wasn't anything unusual, just like we suspected. Following the money won't lead us to the killer in this case."

Frank took a sip of his coffee, digesting the information. For the past six months, they'd been investigating a Balkavian mercenary group operating out of Jacksonville. They had received a tip that something was going down at Cox's office that fateful night. They still hadn't been able to prove any kind of connection, though, between the Balkavians and Cox. In many cases, the money led to the killer, but so far it hadn't in this case. Why had they killed him? Had he just been in the wrong place at the wrong time?

Frank leaned back, his frustration growing. "Nothing new on the computer angle?"

"Nope, nothing out of the ordinary. In fact, there wasn't even that much on it. Looks like his daughter was right—he barely used the thing."

Bailey had been right about something else too— they'd lost a lot of valuable information when those paper files had been stolen. It was unfortunate that the team hadn't thought to grab them on the night of the murder, but they hadn't realized their importance at the time. Now it was too late. "Thanks, Ben. I'm off to interview the applicants. I'll catch up with you again once I have some insight."

"Sounds like a plan."

Frank stirred his coffee as he flipped to the email program on his phone. That was strange. He could see the two messages that Johnson's assistant had sent, but they both showed that they had been read. He pulled out his iPad, and then he also opened his work email account on the off chance that there was something wrong with his phone. It also showed that the two messages had been read, even though he hadn't opened either one of them. Then, right before his eyes, the screen refreshed and both emails were marked Unread.

Frank took a sip of his coffee and a bite of his food as he raised an eyebrow, confused by what he was seeing. Why had the status of the emails changed, and who had changed it? Had someone accessed his account and made the change?

A flash of blue caught his eye and he glanced out the window of the coffee shop. Bailey Cox was just leaving a store across the street. He watched her as she walked toward the bus stop. She looked beautiful, even with that look of grim determination on her face. He glanced up at the sign over the door she had exited. It was an internet café. A sinking feeling hit him hard in the pit of his stomach. He picked up his phone again and called his department's IT specialist.

"IT, Sergeant Daniels."

"This is Detective Franklin Kennedy, badge number 4577. I think my email has just been hacked. Can you run a check for me?" He fed the sergeant the details and then waited a moment for the confirmation. It wasn't long in coming. The knot in his stomach twisted and he grimaced. It looked like he hadn't seen the last of Bailey Cox after all. She had just broken the law. Again.

"It will be just another minute," the secretary said with an apologetic smile. The hospital administration's waiting room wasn't as fancy as the room at Gates, but it was decorated tastefully. Bailey tried to relax, even though it was nearly impossible. She hated hospitals. Her mother had gotten lost in the system, given insufficient treatment because she couldn't afford health insurance. By the time Bailey had stolen the money to make sure her mother got the help she needed, it was too late. It was hard not to hold the entire medical industry responsible for her mother's fate.

To distract herself from the thought of her mother, she focused on the list she'd stolen from Kennedy's email—the names of the applicants that had brought her here.

She didn't know how long it would take Franklin Kennedy to realize she had broken into his email account, if he did at all. Still, she had started her quest to interview the applicants in the middle of the list rather than at the top in hopes of throwing him off if he decided to come after her. If the police wouldn't let her help, then she would solve this murder on her own. She nervously leafed through the stack of magazines and glanced around the room again, making sure Kennedy was nowhere to be seen.

She was also keeping her eyes open for the man in black. Something was off about him, and she had noticed him a second time after she'd left Gates. She wasn't sure, but it looked like he had been watching her as she'd left the internet café. *Creepy.* That was the word for him. At least now he had disappeared and she felt a measure of relief.

A few more minutes passed, and finally the secretary rose and came to her side. "Okay, Dr. Petrela is almost here. Let me take you back to his office." The secretary led her to a nice office filled with medical books and journals and Bailey took a seat. "I'm sorry for the wait," the nurse said in parting.

"It isn't a problem." She'd been waiting for over an hour and a half to see the hospital CEO, but it had been surprising that she'd even gotten her foot in the door. The man was extremely busy, but when she'd explained who she was and why she wanted to meet, the CEO had promised her ten minutes between meetings.

He entered the room a few moments later, and Bailey noted that his internet picture hadn't done justice to the man's square jaw or bright, intelligent eyes. It also hadn't shown the man's size, which was quite substantial. He was a formidable presence, though not a frightening one. His handshake was firm and his smile friendly.

"First, let me say how sorry I was to hear about your father," Dr. Petrela intoned, true sympathy in his eyes.

"Thank you," Bailey answered. "How well did you know him?"

"We'd met for dinner twice. I've applied for the CEO position at Gates, as you know, and Mr. Cox had several questions. You see, I got my advanced degree in Europe, and some of the school records were hard to verify. I'm sure he didn't have any trouble after our interviews, however. I imagine you're continuing the investigation?"

"Yes," she agreed, without correcting his misunderstanding. She *was* investigating. She just wasn't doing it for Gates. "Could you tell me where you went to school, please?"

"Of course. My history isn't a secret. I got my undergraduate and master's degrees at the University of Applied Sciences in Budapest, and then I received my doctorate in Balkavia at the Mirianka University."

Bailey made a note in her phone of his responses. She would check them out later. "And have you lived in the United States for very long?" She could still hear the tiniest hint of an accent when he spoke, but he'd obviously gone to great lengths to eliminate it.

"Going on twenty years now, though I was born here in the US. My family moved overseas when my father was in the military, and once he retired, he decided to stay."

"But not you?" She smiled and he returned the smile.

"No, not me." He shifted some papers on his desk. "My wife is also American, and she wanted to return home so she could be closer to her parents. We've lived here in Jacksonville ever since."

"Why would you like to work at Gates?"

He found a folder with a green tab and handed it to her. "Gates is a mover and shaker in the pharmaceutical industry, and I think their development team is on the cusp of some exciting new medicines. I want to be a part of that. Working at the hospital here has been fulfilling, but I'm mostly administration, and it's time for a change. My application and résumé are in that folder."

Bailey nodded and then motioned to the mini helmet that was on his desk.

"Are you a football fan?"

The CEO laughed and glanced at the helmet. "If I were, I wouldn't admit it," he said in a jovial tone. "The local team hasn't had a winning season since 2007." He motioned with his hands as he spoke. "That helmet was a gift from my daughter. She's a true believer and still harbors hope that they'll make it to the playoffs. I don't suffer from delusions the way she does."

Bailey grinned and glanced at the folder he'd given her. She scanned the contents and asked a few more questions, and then she rose to leave. He had seemed very open, and, so far, she hadn't noticed any red flags. He also seemed at ease during their conversation. On the surface, nothing seemed problematic. She had to get to her computer if she wanted to know more, and that's exactly where she was headed. She offered her hand, knowing that her ten minutes were up. "Thank you so much for your time, Dr. Petrela."

"My pleasure. I hope you are able to get justice for your father."

"So do I."

They shook hands and she stowed the folder and her few belongings in her tote. Then she headed out into the hallway. She was past ready to be free of the hospital. The smells and sights of people suffering continued to flood her with memories of her mother's final days. Despite the addictions, Bailey had still loved her mother. Theirs had been a rocky relationship, but Bailey's last criminal acts had all been about her mother's care. As she'd watched her mother's body wither away from lung cancer, Bailey had gotten more and more desperate to get her mother the help she needed.

It had all been a wasted effort, however. Right after she had committed her crimes, started paying the bills and brought the equipment home, she'd found her mother collapsed on the bathroom floor—the result of both her coughing and a heroin overdose. Bailey's efforts had been too little too late, and when the officers had come to investigate the scene, they'd found the stolen equipment before she'd even thought to hide it. Her lack of foresight had cost her mightily. Her mother had died shortly after Bailey's arrest. Bailey hadn't even had a chance to say good-bye.

Bailey rubbed her eyes, trying to erase the memories. She had been such a mess back then. It hadn't even occurred to her that she had done something wrong with her thefts. Her only thought had been to save her mother.

She liked to think that she'd learned her lesson in jail. Even better, she'd become a Christian during her college days and had slowly gotten on the right track. But changes didn't just happen overnight. She still made blunders here and there, and she was already coming to regret her latest mistake. Hacking Kennedy's email had been a stupid, impetuous display of bad judgment. She just hoped she could avoid him for the foreseeable future until she could track down her father's killer. Maybe he wouldn't care if she could get results from her own investigation.

She pulled out the list from her tote bag and put a check mark by Dr. Petrela's name. It was time to move on to the next applicant. She still had a few daylight hours left and could probably interview one more applicant on the list today if she hurried. Gabriel Jeffries, an entrepreneur who worked from his beach house, was next. He had already agreed to see her if she could be at his place by 4:00 p.m. She had just enough time to make it.

"You know, most people start at the top of the list, not the middle."

Her breath caught in her throat as she recognized the voice. She spun around as dread swept over her. Franklin Kennedy stood only a few feet away, nonchalantly leaning against the wall. He smiled at her, but it was an ominous smile, and she knew she was in trouble.

"What are you doing here?"

"Looking for you," he said quietly. "I'm having some trouble with my email and thought maybe you would be able to help."

"Doesn't sound like a very serious problem. I'm sure your IT folks can fix it for you."

Kennedy shook his head. "Actually, it's a much bigger problem than most people realize. It's a felony to hack a governmental email account. Were you aware of that?"

Bailey didn't think. She took one step backward and then another. Then she turned and ran.

SIX

The hallway was crowded, and several people shouted as she made her escape. A nurse pushing a cart with a computer was up ahead and Bailey quickly made it around her and shoved at the cart, not stopping to see if it actually blocked the hallway or not. She skidded to a halt and pushed an empty gurney behind her in another effort to slow Kennedy down and then turned down a new hallway.

She dared not look, but she could feel that he wasn't very far behind. The fear was palpable and her heart was throbbing in her chest. Had the cluttered hallway and the people slowed him down enough? Would she actually have a chance to escape? The side doors of the hospital were in sight and hope surged.

"Sheriff's department!" Kennedy shouted after her. "Don't let her get away!"

A hand snarled out and gripped her arm, but she yanked it away and took a few more steps before another man grabbed her shoulder.

Again, she pulled free, but the delay had cost her.

Kennedy was only a few feet away as she hit the door and spun out onto the parking deck. She darted out into the humid air and aimed for the staircase that led down to the bottom level.

The tackle caught her by surprise. One moment she was running; the next, his arms locked around her shoulders, knocking her to the ground. The air left her body with a whoosh and she clamored for breath as she felt him fall on top of her. Even so, she wasn't quite ready to surrender. He was so big that it was hard to fight against him, but she still tried to pull away, even though, deep down, she knew it was a wasted effort. He quickly straddled her from behind, grabbed her right hand and pulled it roughly behind her. She felt the click of the handcuffs and knew there was no escaping. She heard the final click of the metal and her body sagged. How was she going to solve her father's murder now?

Kennedy pulled her to her feet and then immediately reached down and took her pistol from her ankle holster and stashed it in his waistband. She only had the one weapon with her today. He led her back toward the hospital doors until he reached her tote bag, lying on the ground where she had carelessly discarded it. His grip on her arm was tight—almost painful—and she could see the anger and disappointment warring for supremacy on his face. He reached down and grabbed the bag, and then he did a quick search of the contents. He pulled out the printed copy of his email from Gates, shook his head and then turned her to face him. She had a hard time looking him in the eye but finally raised her head. He held the proof right in his hands. There was no use denying her actions. It was all she could do to hold her ground under his intense scrutiny. He was so close she could see the dark flecks in his eyes. "You just won't take no for an answer, will you?"

She pursed her lips together, fighting the impulse to say something pithy. It was her own fault she was in this mess, and on some level she knew that, but right now all of her anger was directed at him. Still, it was better to keep her mouth shut and not incriminate herself further. She tried to look away from him, but he moved into her field of vision, forcing the confrontation.

"You're unbelievable," he said tightly. "I thought you said you'd changed."

Okay. After that, even superglue couldn't help her keep her mouth shut. "He was my father," she responded with a glare, "and you refused to let me help. What did you expect?"

Frank snorted. He'd hoped that Bailey Cox had truly changed as she'd claimed, but it was obvious that she still had no regard for the law. He tried not to let his frustration show. "I expected you to follow the law and not hack my email account. I expected you to quit committing felonies. Silly me. I guess I was expecting the impossible. A zebra can't change her stripes." He looked into her eyes for any sign of repentance, but what he saw was a vulnerability that he didn't expect. The look she gave him almost made him feel guilty. Was he pushing too hard? She had just lost her father. And yet the law was the law, and she had broken into an official state computer server. This wasn't a game they were playing. Her actions had serious consequences.

He considered taking her back in the direction they'd come, but bystanders were already starting to gather and he didn't want Bailey to become a spectacle. Instead he turned and started walking her toward the exit. His car was parked below and it wouldn't take them too long to reach it.

Frank's thoughts continued to ramble. As far as he was concerned, Bailey's escape attempt was evidence of a guilty conscience, and the copy of his email in her bag was incontrovertible proof. She had surprised him by starting her interviews in the middle of the applicant list instead of at the top, but by making a few quick phone calls, it hadn't been hard to find her. Her actions might have been justified in her mind, but they were also a third-degree felony.

"You have the right to remain silent, Bailey Cox. If you give up that right, anything you say can and will be used against you. You have the right to an attorney."

"Save it," Bailey said gruffly. "I've heard it all before."

Her sarcasm made him angry. No, he was more than angry. He was bitterly disappointed. This whole situation bothered him on too many levels to count. "Yes, you have, haven't you?" he said quietly. Once again, she had thrown away her future. With her criminal record, her sentence this time could be substantial. And for what? All she had to do was stay out of the way and let him do his job.

They finished going down the stairs and Frank led

her toward his car. The closer they got, the more she dragged her feet. As they made it to the concrete, he was half dragging, half carrying her along the sidewalk. "Come on, Bailey. Quit fighting me."

"I can't go back to prison, Kennedy." Her voice was suddenly desperate, as if the weight of her decision had finally started to sink in.

"You should have thought of that sooner—before you hacked into an official law enforcement database. They don't just slap your hand for that."

"Can you prove I did it?"

"Can you give me another plausible explanation for that email I found in your bag, or for why you're here, interviewing applicants whom you have no other way of knowing about?" He was secretly pleased when she kept silent, not attempting to sell him some tall tale. Bailey Cox was a lot of things, but she had never been a liar. She wasn't evil or malicious. She just made a lot of very bad choices with serious consequences.

Another pang of regret hit him. The last time he had arrested her, her mother died. This time he was arresting her after her father's death. This really was a messy, horrible situation. When he spoke, his tone was sincere. "I'm sorry, Bailey. This is not the way I wanted this to turn out." They reached his car and he opened the back door.

"I'm sorry too, Detective Kennedy." Her voice was pleading now. "I made a mistake—a bad one. I realize that now. Please don't do this."

Their eyes met and he saw tears swimming in the blue depths. He'd seen a lot of tears from arrested criminals over the years, but, for some reason, these really affected him. He'd always had a soft spot for Bailey. He couldn't or wouldn't examine those feelings, however, especially not now. He had a job to do. That was the bottom line. He didn't see shades of gray in the law and didn't make exceptions. "I don't have a choice." He started to put her in the back seat, but she pulled against him. He put his hand on her head and tried to guide her in so she wouldn't bump against the door frame, but she continued to fight him.

"I'll tell you about the money!" she blurted out quickly.

Frank stopped. Had he just heard correctly? Was she really offering him a chance to close that case, the one that had been nagging him for the last six years?

He pulled her up in front of him and turned her around so he could see her face. He searched for veracity in her eyes. "What exactly are you offering?"

"Your wish come true, Detective Kennedy. Look, let's make a deal. You don't arrest me yet—*and* you let me work the investigation with you. In exchange, as soon as the murderer is arrested, I'll give myself up voluntarily so you can charge me for hacking your email—and I'll tell you where the rest of the money is. That's what you've wanted all along, isn't it?"

He raised an eyebrow. Plea bargains happened every day in the justice system. But would she really follow through? "What's the catch? Are you going to try to disappear as soon as the arrest is made?"

"I give you my word that I won't."

"And I'm supposed to trust a convicted felon?"

"I haven't lied to you yet."

Her words struck home. Hadn't he just been thinking about that? Yet trusting her seemed almost impossible.

"Look, I know this goes against the grain for you, but I'm only after one thing here—justice for my father. Once that's done, you can throw the book at me if that's what you want." Her chin was trembling and she was making a valiant effort to keep the tears at bay as she spoke as convincingly as she could.

"Putting you behind bars is not my goal, Bailey. This isn't about trying to fill up the prisons. It's about right and wrong. What I want is for you to turn over that stolen money and stop committing crimes because it's the right thing to do, not as a bargaining chip." He let out a breath, still considering her offer.

"It's not always that black-and-white," she whispered.

"It is to me. Crime is the easy choice. Doing things the right way with integrity—that's the hard part."

She drew her lips into a thin line, again choosing to stay quiet rather than argue. It was a wise move on her part and one he respected.

There was a lot he admired about Bailey. But could he trust her? With a new prison sentence hanging over her head, would she really do what she was promising? He wanted to believe her and give her the benefit of the doubt. He also really wanted to get that money back and close that case. In the end, giving her a second chance won out. "Alright, Bailey, you've got a deal. But you're sticking by my side until this case is closed. No running. Got it?"

She nodded, her expression one of relief. "Thank you, Detective Kennedy. You won't be sorry. I promise."

He turned her around and unlocked the handcuffs, surprised that she had even bothered to use his title. "I'm already sorry."

SEVEN

Franklin Kennedy glanced again in his rearview mirror. They were on their way to interview Gabriel Jeffries but had picked up the tail shortly after leaving the hospital. The black sedan was still only a few cars back and had been following them for more than fifteen minutes. He slowed and made a turn to the left. Sure enough, the black sedan stayed with them. He called in the tail on his radio, hoping there was a cruiser somewhere nearby that could intercept their follower before something happened.

"What's going on?" Bailey asked, turning to see what had captured his attention.

"There's a car back there tailing us—a black four-door." He suddenly jerked the car into the passing lane. "Get down!"

Bailey obeyed, just as the first bullet ripped into the seat by her shoulder. She screamed as the second bullet cracked the windshield. She tried to wedge herself lower against the car seat. Frank didn't wait for the third. He gunned the engine and tried to put as much distance as he could between them and the sedan. The other car dropped back a bit due to Frank's speed, but within moments it was back again, and the gunman was again holding his pistol out of the window and pointing it at them.

Instead of speeding up, this time Frank suddenly slowed and the black car jolted ahead of them. Frank slowed even further and took a hard right down a side road. The tires screeched in protest as the back of the car fishtailed on some loose gravel.

"Did you lose him?" Bailey asked as she started to get back in her seat.

"Stay down!" he said tightly, pushing her lower. "He's gone for now, but he'll be back in no time." He got on his radio again, updated the dispatch about the situation and then stomped on the gas. Suddenly the black sedan swung back behind them from a side street, and another bullet shattered the rear window of the car. Frank muttered under his breath and maneuvered around a large truck that shielded them temporarily from the onslaught. He took the opportunity to spin into a U-turn. The tires squealed against the pavement, but he kept the car on the road. He checked the rearview mirror and saw the black car was still in pursuit but had dropped back. It was slowly gaining on them but had gotten stuck behind an antique VW Bug and a minivan. He hadn't been able to see who was driving, but he did note that the man was Caucasian with dark hair.

Frank glanced over at Bailey, who was still scrunched against the seats. "Hold on. We're going to try to put

some distance between us and the guy with the gun."
He punched the accelerator and felt the engine surge.

Bailey glanced up at him and, even though there was
fear mirrored there, Frank also saw a level of trust. The
look surprised him. He might decide to analyze it later,
but right now all he wanted to think about was getting
away from that black car. He heard sirens in the distance, and the dispatcher told him help was only a few
blocks away.

Frank took another look in his rearview mirror. The
black car finally passed the two slower vehicles. He saw
the gun come out of the driver's side window once again
as the perpetrator fired at them. Frank felt one shot hit
the back of the car and the second hit higher, near the
roof. He swerved to miss the flying bullets and the tires
skidded in response, but he managed to keep control
of the wheel. Despite his maneuvering, another bullet
caught the back side of the vehicle near the trunk. The
man fired one last shot that missed, and then pulled
his arm back inside the window. Without warning, the
black sedan zagged onto a side road, abandoning the
chase. It didn't take Frank long to figure out why—two
police cars were coming up fast behind them, lights and
sirens blazing.

"Need some help, Detective, or should we follow the
perp?" a deep male voice asked over the police radio.

Frank glanced at Bailey and she nodded at him.
"We're good. Stay with the perp." He slowed and, after
another couple of miles, pulled to the side of the road
and parked. Then he motioned toward the seat. "Okay,
Bailey. Looks like we're safe." She pulled herself up

and fingered the hole in the upholstery, where a bullet had missed her by inches. He met her eye. "Are you sure you're okay?"

Her eyes were wide. "Yeah."

"I'll take you home now."

"No!" she said suddenly. "We're both in one piece. And Gabriel Jeffries is still waiting to see us and we're only a few minutes away. I'll pull myself together during the ride over." She brushed some of the broken glass off her shirt.

Her comments made him smile in spite of himself. Her skin was a pasty white and her hands were still shaking, but she wanted to push on. He admired her spirit. Even though he found it appealing, however, her bravado still wasn't enough to make him restart the engine. "I have to report this event, turn in the car..."

"Look, they arrested the guy who was shooting at us, right? I heard it on your radio."

"Yeah, they got him."

"So we should be safe. And you can do all that paperwork and deal with the car after the interview," she pleaded. "We've come this far. Jeffries might have the answers we need."

He thought about the group of Balkavians they were investigating. Even though one had been caught, they had dossiers on three others, not to mention the two who had killed Bailey's father. And there was no telling how many more were involved. "Someone knows we're investigating this case and is trying to stop us. It probably goes way beyond that one man who was shooting at our car. Don't you realize somebody just tried to kill us?"

"Of course. Don't *you* realize those men already succeeded at killing my father?"

Frank took a moment to consider her words. She
made a valid point. And she was right—he could do
the paperwork and deal with the car after the interview.
He glanced at his watch. It went against his better judgment, but he was as anxious as she was to break a lead
in the case. "Alright, let's get this done."

He pulled back onto the road, heading toward the address for Gabriel Jeffries, the fourth person on Gates's
list. He turned his focus to the job at hand. They found
the house and parked. Once they knocked, they were
escorted back to a wide back porch, where the man was
sitting under a large umbrella, working on a laptop and
sipping a frozen drink. Mr. Jeffries was wearing white
linen clothing and barely seemed to be sweating, even
though the temperature had to be in the mid-90s. He
stood when they arrived and gave them a smile. The
man acted surprised that Bailey was being accompa-
nied by a cop rather than coming alone, but he seemed
to take the change in stride.

"Bailey Cox and Detective Kennedy, is it? Welcome
to my home."

Frank gave the man a brief overview of what they
were doing, and the entrepreneur smiled and nodded.
"Of course, I totally understand. I'm so sorry to hear
about Mr. Cox's demise. Any relation?" He nodded toward Bailey.

"My father," she answered softly.

Frank was once again struck by how inappropriate it
was to have a victim's relative joining him for the inter-

view, but the promised prize of her stolen money was a carrot he couldn't ignore. Besides, he still worried she'd run, and the only way he could keep an eye on her was to keep her close. His actions weren't against the rules. He'd worked with several confidential informants who traded information for a reduced sentence, but this time felt different. Since Bailey was the daughter of the victim, his methods might raise some eyebrows. He imagined his boss would have some choice comments about his actions if this whole thing went south. He pushed those concerns aside. It would all be worth it if he could recover the stolen money and finally close that older case that was the bane of his existence.

"Ah, again, I am sorry."

Bailey nodded as Frank leaned forward. "Can you tell us why you're interested in working for Gates, Mr. Jeffries?" He motioned around him. "You seem to already have a dream job and a wonderful home."

Mr. Jeffries smiled. "Thank you. Indeed, I do love my work, but Gates offers entirely new challenges. It's an exciting opportunity. They're already international, but I see them expanding into more markets. Gates is a quality company and produces several excellent products. They're going places, and I want to drive that train."

Frank felt like he was being sold a used car. The man's enthusiasm was over the top. Frank hadn't had a chance to do much searching into the man's background yet, but he wondered if Jeffries was really all that he appeared.

A potted plant on the railing suddenly exploded,

spraying them with dirt, and Frank jumped as a second bullet dug into the wood just a few inches below the pot. Somebody was shooting at them again, but this time using a semiautomatic weapon with a silencer! Before he could even react, the third bullet hit Jeffries, followed quickly by a fourth that entered the man's forehead, killing him instantly.

EIGHT

Bailey screamed and her eyes widened in shock. She sat frozen in place.

"Get down!" Frank yelled, grabbing Bailey and pushing her to the deck floor. There were some wooden benches nearby and he kicked them over and then quickly moved Bailey and himself behind them. He knew a high-powered rifle could still penetrate the wood, but it was the closest viable shelter he could find. He grabbed his radio and called in the shooting, asking for immediate backup, as well.

Once he was done with the call, he looked quickly through the bench slats, his gun drawn, hoping to catch sight of the shooter. He knew his pistol had nowhere near the range of the high-powered rifle, but it was all he had with him.

"Stay behind me, Bailey. Do you hear me? Don't move unless I tell you to." Two more bullets hit the wood about five inches above his head and the bench shook with the force.

Bailey didn't answer him, but he felt her lay a hand

on his back in response. In an odd sort of way, her touch strengthened him. He crawled toward the end of the bench. Another bullet hit inches from his chest, splintering the wood. The next bullet whizzed by his ear and covered him in shards of plaster from the stucco on the side of the house. He was effectively pinned down. He still couldn't see his shooter, and he couldn't move and pursue the gunman without fear of drawing more fire. His eyes darted from the stand of palm trees to the house in the distance. There were two balconies and a back patio area, but he didn't see a living soul. He turned toward the beach, but dunes and waves were all he saw.

They were stuck. There was nothing he could do until backup arrived or the danger decreased. The helplessness left him feeling frustrated and angry. He heard a soft cry behind him and crawled back to Bailey's side.

"Are you hurt?"

"No." Her eyes were large and she was staring straight in front of her. He followed her line of vision and could see Gabriel Jeffries's face quite clearly. He still had a look of surprise splashed across his features, and he was lying in a pool of blood. "Bailey? Bailey, look away." She still seemed locked in position, as if unable to move. He gently touched her chin and turned her face. "Keep your eyes on me, not him. Got it? Keep your eyes right here." He motioned with two of his fingers toward his face. She glanced at him, but then her eyes moved back to Jeffries. Frank again softly repositioned her head away from the sight. There was still a glazed look of horror on her face. She shook her head.

"I've never seen someone die before," she whispered, her hand moving to her throat.

"And, Lord willing, you'll never see it again, either." He pulled her close, resting her head against his chest. In his line of work, he'd seen several horrible sights, but Bailey should never have had to see this, especially with her father's death still plaguing her mind. He rubbed her back in a soothing motion, but he could still hear her quiet sobs. He pulled her closer. He was second-guessing the deal he'd made with her now that she'd been shot at twice in one day. He knew she didn't want to go back to jail, but he couldn't help feeling she'd be safer there right now. He said a silent prayer, asking God to comfort her and help erase the terrible images from her mind.

A few moments later he heard sirens arriving from a distance, and shortly after that, he heard movement in the house. He turned and pointed his gun at the doorway, just in case.

"Frankie? Is that you?"

Frank instantly recognized Ben Graham's voice. He lowered his gun and smiled.

"Ben? You sure took your time getting here. What'd you do, ride your bike?"

Ben stepped out on the porch and smiled in return. "Can't help it. I was still trying to sort out the mess you left behind you on the road. Your car looks like Swiss cheese, by the way." He helped Frank to his feet. "The area is clear. We found a couple of brass cartridges where the shooter had been, but he's long gone and appears to have been by himself. He was out on the beach, hiding behind the dunes." He wiped his brow and made a sweeping motion with his hands. "You two okay?"

Frank turned and helped Bailey stand. Her entire body was still shaking like a leaf. "We are now. Bailey, these guys are good at their jobs. If they say it's safe, then it's safe." She nodded and took several steps away from the scene, her arms wrapped around her middle. Her face was a pasty white and, for a minute, she looked like she was about to throw up. He moved her away from Jeffries's body so it was out of her field of vision and took her to the steps that led down to the beach. He wanted to comfort her, but he also had a job to do. "Look, please sit here and just hang on. I've got to work the scene, but I'll be back to get you in a little bit. There are plenty of law enforcement officers out here now, so you should be perfectly safe. Okay?"

She nodded at him with her big blue eyes and he felt a knot twist in his gut. Would she still be there when he was finished? He second-guessed himself once again. Was he making a huge mistake here by agreeing to let her help with the investigation? Was he wrong to believe her promise not to escape? And even if she was trustworthy, did he trust *himself* to keep her safe? Someone had made it abundantly clear that they were targets, as well. Would he be able to live with himself if she got hurt on his watch?

He pushed the questions from his mind and returned to Ben and the rest of his team. There would be time later for ruminations. For now, he needed to focus on the case.

Ben met him at the door, his eyebrow raised and his voice soft. "Hey, isn't that Bailey Cox?"

"Yep."

"Should I ask?"

"Nope."

"Alright, then."

Frank was instantly grateful for his excellent relationship with his team. There was a level of trust there, and while Frank knew that at some point he would have to explain his relationship with Bailey, for now, they wouldn't press him.

"So who is the victim?" Ben asked, changing the subject.

Frank explained the highlights of the investigation to date, leaving out the part about Bailey's arrest. "I think we need to notify the rest of the applicants to take extra precautions. At first, I wasn't sure Gates was connected to Cox's death, but now the connection seems impossible to ignore. I'm not sure exactly what's going on here yet, but somebody didn't want us talking to Gabriel Jeffries, and I'll bet they didn't want him taking that job at Gates, either. He was their top contender."

Graham nodded. "I've got uniforms over at both neighbors' houses, taking statements and looking around, but the beach was apparently blocked off about two hundred yards in each direction with fake signs that prohibited trespassing. We're canvasing the area, just in case someone saw who cordoned off the area or got a glimpse of the shooter, but so far no leads."

"Where'd you find the shells?"

"Southeast of the boardwalk. Looks like the shooter was lying prone in the sand."

"Maybe forensics will find us a fingerprint on the bullet casings," Frank said hopefully.

"I wouldn't count on it," Ben said, his tone low. "This shooter seems like a professional, and the casings came from a weapon that the Balkavians favor."

Frank knew Ben was right. But how did this all fit together? Why did a gang of Balkavian thugs care who Gates hired? Was the CEO position, or any job for that matter, worth killing over?

It took another two hours before Frank was finished with his work and ready to go. By that time, the coroner had come and gone, as well as the crime scene forensics team. When Frank finally had a chance to go looking for Bailey, he didn't see her where he had left her. Fear instantly swelled in his chest. Had she run, despite her promise to stay? He took a look in both directions down the beach, but saw no sign of her.

So she had lied to him after all. He could kick himself for being so gullible. Of course she would disappear the first chance she got. That way she could go live with her stolen money and avoid a jail cell. He put his hands on his hips and fisted his hands. What an idiot he had been! How could he have trusted her? Would he never learn his lesson?

A uniformed officer approached him with an apologetic demeanor. "Ah, Detective?"

"Yeah, what do you want?" His tone was gruffer than it needed to be, and he was instantly sorry for snapping at the younger officer.

"Are you looking for the woman who was sitting here before?"

Frank turned and got a better look at the man. He didn't recognize him. "Yes, that's who I'm looking for. Did you see what happened to her?"

"Ah, actually, I did. She came and asked me to tell you that she needed some fresh air away from the house and she was going to sit on the beach. She said she'd meet you out there when you were done working the crime scene. I meant to tell you earlier, but it's been kinda crazy around here."

Frank felt his face turning red. He had jumped to conclusions with such swiftness that his head was still spinning. "Thanks. Do you know if she went right or left?"

The officer nodded quickly and pointed to the left. "She went that way, sir."

Bailey was tired of walking, so she'd found a some-what shady area on the beach away from the crowd and had plopped down in the sand, completely ignoring the fact that she was still dressed in her fancy clothes. She'd already been on the ground twice today, and the condition of her outfit was the absolute last thing on her mind. She couldn't believe she'd been shot at twice today, and images of Jeffries's death still filled her mind's eye. It would be a while before she forgot what happened, if she ever could. She tried to focus on the waves instead and the sound of the water hitting the sand. The beach was beautiful, especially with the sky just starting to change into evening colors of blues and pinks, yet the lovely scene did nothing to erase the horrific images.

"So here's where you ended up."

The voice caught her by surprise and she shielded her eyes against the sun as she looked up toward Kennedy. He looked tired but at the same time more relieved and relaxed than she had seen him all day. He had even removed his tie and jacket and his shirt sleeves were rolled up. She was actually glad to get a glimpse of this side of him. It made him seem more approachable, more human. Until now, she couldn't ever remember seeing him without his tie. Franklin Kennedy always exuded professionalism and perfection, even though he really wasn't that much older than she was—maybe five or six years? He'd been a young rookie cop when they'd first met. She'd been sixteen, and he'd been twenty-two or so. It seemed so long ago. So much had changed.

She glanced at his face and tried to smile. "Sorry for not staying on the steps. I just had to get away from the madness, you know?"

He stood there for a moment, as if he wasn't sure what his next move should be, but he finally sat down next to her on the sand. "Yes, I totally understand. That's why I think we need to reevaluate our agreement. It's not safe for you to continue with the investigation. I don't want you to get hurt. Today was too close for comfort."

Her eyes widened. "No! I want to keep going. I'm aware of the risks and I accept them. Do you want me to sign something? I will, you know. I'll do whatever it takes to ride this to the end. This case is really important to me."

He sighed. "More important than your life?"

Bailey ignored his comment. "I could carry my gun again if you'd let me. Then I could protect myself."

He shook his head. "First of all, a pistol is no good against a high-powered rifle, and second, that's simply not going to happen. You're a convicted felon."

"Who had her rights restored and was able to qualify for a concealed weapons permit in the state of Florida. I'm legal to carry."

"Who also just broke into a government server, stole private documents and committed a third-degree felony. I'm not going to bend on this, Bailey. No gun."

"Okay, fine, but I'm not going to quit," she said fiercely. "I'm going to find out who murdered my father. You could make it harder for me, but I won't stop, no matter what you or anybody else does." She met his eye, trying to show him her determination.

He had an odd look on his face that she couldn't quite decipher. She regarded him closely and for the first time saw him as a person instead of a law enforcement officer bent on her destruction. There was true concern in his eyes and even an aura of protectiveness that she had never felt directed toward her before. She suddenly understood that he was looking out for her, not trying to sabotage her plans. The realization surprised her.

She'd always seen Kennedy as the enemy—the adversary who wanted nothing more than to put her behind bars and was just waiting for her to make a mistake. This man before her seemed like a totally different person. Yes, he was watching her, but he was genuinely worried about her safety.

His concern touched her. She'd had very few close friends during her life and could count on one hand the number of people who had actually cared about her. Hers was a lonely existence, but she'd discovered over the years that she did better on her own without leaning on anybody else. She'd been unable to rely on her parents, and she had rarely dated or formed close friendships. The computer was her world, and it was easy to get lost in cyberspace in a sea of anonymity. It was safer that way. If she didn't get close to anyone, she couldn't get hurt.

She continued to watch Kennedy carefully as he considered his options. It was almost as if he were checking off a pro and con list in his head. In the end, she must have convinced him, because he stood and brushed the sand off of his pants. "Okay, Bailey Cox. Let's find you a computer so we can get to work." He offered her his hand and she grasped it firmly as he helped her to her feet. She thought about the events of the day and searched for something to be thankful for. Was she thankful for Kennedy being in her life? That one she'd have to think about. The answer seemed to change daily.

His grip was tight and he held on to her for a moment longer than expected before releasing her. Their eyes met again, and she saw that he would do everything he could to keep her safe. His hands were warm and strong and she found herself enjoying the comfort in his touch. She studied him for a few moments more and felt she saw him with fresh eyes. Maybe he wasn't the enemy after all. Maybe there was more to Franklin Kennedy than she had ever realized. The thought left her with a strangely odd but wonderful feeling, and she let the warmth sweep over her, not quite sure how to react.

"Lead the way, Detective."

NINE

Frank opened the door to his apartment and stepped aside so Bailey could enter. It felt really odd to be inviting her into his home just hours after arresting her, but after his scare this afternoon in the car and at the beach, he wanted to keep an eye on her—awkward or not. He didn't want her to disappear on him.

He was also seriously worried about her safety. There were already two people dead—and although he didn't understand the connection yet, he knew instinctively that everything that had happened was related to both the Balkavian case and Gates Industries. Whether she realized it or not, Bailey was involved in this case up to her neck, and he was going to protect her. He didn't want a third murder on his hands, and he also didn't trust her to stay out of trouble.

They had swung by Bailey's apartment to pack a small suitcase and grab her computer, and once inside his own apartment, Frank showed her the guest room and then encouraged her to set up her computer on the kitchen table while he made dinner. They hadn't seen anybody following them, but Frank had arranged for a patrol to swing by his apartment every few hours, just in case. As Bailey started hooking things up, he pulled out the fixings for omelets and laid out a variety of items on his countertop.

"Anything special you want in your omelet?" he asked, motioning to the choices on the counter.

Bailey eyed the ingredients hungrily. He wondered if she had eaten today. "Tomato, black olives, cheddar cheese and a little garlic, maybe?"

"You got it." He pulled out the egg carton and a small bowl and started cracking the eggs as he tried to decide what seasonings would go best with her choices. He wasn't a gourmet, but he did like to spend time in the kitchen—even if some of his creations left even him with raised eyebrows after the first bite. Everything usually came out tasting pretty good, but his mixtures of spices and ingredients were often an afterthought or a spur-of-the-moment idea. Although he lived most of his life in an orderly fashion with strict adherence to the rules, cooking was the one avenue where creativity was king and he refused to follow the recipe.

Frank looked up from his work and saw Bailey connect to the internet with the password he'd provided and start typing furiously on her keyboard. He marveled at her skill and was even a tad envious. He didn't know coding or computer languages and didn't have the intrinsic talent Bailey displayed at the keyboard. She had started off self-taught, which made her skills even more astounding. He was also amazed at Bailey's ability to quickly analyze what she was seeing, find the holes and make the fixes necessary to achieve her objective. In some ways, they didn't even speak the same language. Her talent and skill were remarkable.

She typed some more and then pushed back from the table with a thoughtful look on her face. She pointed at some large Post-it brand flip chart pads that he had stored against the wall. "Can we use those to take notes? I think better if I can see everything laid out in front of me. I would normally do it on my computer, but that would make it hard for you to see."

Frank nodded. "Absolutely. I was hoping they'd come in handy someday. They're left over from a presentation I did on gun safety a while back."

"Got any markers?"

"There're a few in a box in the cabinet. Top left drawer."

He started on the omelets while she took three of the sheets from one of the pads and posted them on his dining room wall. She found the markers and drew a timeline of her father's murder across the top, and added the information they had discovered about his death. Then she listed each of the Gates's applicants' names and what they knew to date about each of them.

So far, the murdered Gabriel Jeffries and Dr. Petrela, the hospital CEO she had interviewed, were the only ones they knew much about. Frank hadn't had a chance to interview the doctor, so he listened carefully as she recounted and recorded what she'd learned during the interview. He had to admit that she had been rather thorough. She taped the doctor's résumé under his name as well and a few other details she'd gleaned about the other candidates. When she'd hacked his email, she'd gotten not only the list of applicants but also her father's preliminary report on each of them, which would save them valuable time. He watched as she sheepishly pulled out the report and then started adding notes from that document, as well.

Finally, he was done cooking the meal and he slid a plate with a perfectly cooked omelet in front of her. "Coffee? Tea?"

"Water is great. Wow. This is some fantastic omelet," she said after sampling the first bite. Her body language made it evident that she wasn't giving false praise. She really liked it.

He took a bite of his own omelet and smiled in satisfaction. He had to admit they had come out very well. He watched Bailey as she consumed hers with gusto. For some reason he couldn't quite explain, he was pleased that she was enjoying his cooking. He had shared his passion of the culinary arts with very few. If nothing else, it felt good to have his skills appreciated.

"So where'd you learn to cook?"

Frank raised an eyebrow, surprised at the question. It was the first time she'd asked him something personal, and she seemed genuinely interested. Still he hesitated before speaking. He hadn't quite defined their relationship in his mind just yet, and he wasn't sure how much he wanted to share. Finally, he shrugged. Keeping secrets wasn't in his nature. Franklin Kennedy had always been a down-to-earth kind of guy. With him, what you saw was what you got. "I'm a bachelor and a cop. I can't afford to eat out all the time, but I like to eat well so I had to learn on my own. I've actually taken a few

classes and done a lot of experimenting." He straight-
ened and then shrugged. "I guess I find cooking relaxing too, and if I get a good meal out of it, then I'm
even better off." He paused a moment and watched her
enthusiastically finish off her omelet. It felt strange to
be discussing his hobbies with her, but he felt at ease
with Bailey, despite their history. He knew intrinsically
that she wouldn't criticize or judge him; even if he'd
passed her a plate with something strangely flavored
or burned along the edges, she would still have appreciated his efforts.

He thought about their past for a moment, remembering the first day he had seen her. Although her clothes
had been cheap, she had thrown together an outfit that
made her look rather chic. She had always had an air
of self-confidence during their encounters. It was her
smile that he remembered most, however. She had a
wide, contagious smile that day, even though she had
been rambling fast, trying to talk her way out of trouble.
Six students at the local high school had mysteriously
had their grades changed for the better on the school's
computer system, and he had been tasked with investigating the crime.

Although Bailey had covered her tracks on the computer, the other circumstantial evidence had nailed
her. She'd had $600 cash in her pocket she couldn't
explain, which was the exact amount that the students
had claimed to have paid her, and she'd already been ac-
cused of hacking into the school's attendance program
and erasing her own unexcused absences. Two of her
customers had also volunteered to testify against her,

and as a result, she had gotten a quick and decisive introduction to the juvenile justice system.

Little did Frank know that he would bump into her time and time again over the next few years as she became more and more familiar with the courts through her various escapades. Her computer work was flawless and untraceable, but she always seemed to make other mistakes, like she had just done with him by keeping the printed versions of the stolen emails in her tote bag. Those little mistakes had always been her downfall. A new thought hit him out of the blue. Had she subconsciously wanted to get caught? He didn't know her well enough to say for sure, but her history did make him wonder.

"Well, you've impressed me," she said thoughtfully as she took her empty plate over to the sink, washed it and put it in the rack. Her words broke into his woolgathering and brought him back into the present. "I never pegged you as a guy who liked cooking."

"There's a lot you don't know about me."

"Obviously." She glanced around the room, perusing her surroundings. She spent a moment studying the fishing and diving pictures on his walls. Slowly her attention moved to his coffee table that was actually a lobster trap with a glass top, and his lamp on the end table that had several shells embedded in the mosaic. "I didn't know you liked to fish, either."

"Can you live in Florida and not like fishing?" he asked with a grin.

"I've done just fine without a pole in my hands," she quipped. "Finished?" When he nodded, she took his plate and washed it too, as well as the pan and other dishes he had used. He was delighted with her thoughtfulness. A few minutes later, she came back to the table, opened her laptop again and hit a few keys that brought the machine to life. "'Lay on, Macduff.' What's the first thing you want to research?"

He smiled at the *Macbeth* reference. Apparently, she'd learned something in college after all. "Well, I had Detective Graham contact the other folks on the list to ask them to take security precautions, and he also let them know that we'd be contacting them soon to interview them. I want to start with David Fredericks tomorrow. We can drive up to see him in Atlanta. The only female on the list, Clarissa Merritt, is a local, and the last one, Marty Entemann, is a doctor in a group practice in St. Augustine. If we get back from Atlanta early enough, we can try to interview one of them, as well."

He paused and took a drink from his sweet tea. "Your father did a good job of laying out the basic facts on each of the applicants. It's going to really give us a jump start on the investigation. Don't you agree?"

She looked at him with her big blue eyes and refused to comment, apparently thinking that it was wise not to dwell on the stolen documents. She was pretty good at keeping her mouth shut when it suited her. The look she gave him made his gut twist in a knot once again. Why was he noticing the way her eyes were the color of the ocean after a storm? They were beautiful and an excellent mirror that reflected her thoughts. Bailey had always been easy to read. He liked the way her eyes sparked when she was angry and the way they lit up when she was happy. Now she was calm, but her eyes had a challenge, almost as if she was daring him to prove her guilt regarding the stolen emails. Yet, her guilt wasn't in question. They both knew that she had broken into the department's server and her actions had given her away.

Frank looked deeper, and this time he saw the vulnerability again in Bailey's eyes. He suddenly realized that, under that challenge, she was scared, and her toughness was just a front. The knot in his stomach twisted harder. Why was he noticing so much about her? He needed to take a step back. He tried to push the thoughts away and focus on the job at hand.

"Let's see what we can find out about Fredericks first. What pops up when you Google him?"

"Looks like Fredericks is an oncologist and runs his own office on the north side of Atlanta." She hit a few more keys. "He's been in business for about six years. Before that, he was running a cancer clinic, so it looks like he has a background in administration."

"Yeah, that tracks with your father's report. What else?"

Her fingers flew over the keyboard. "He's single, only has a few friends on his Facebook page, doesn't seem to have any extended family, has expensive tastes in restaurants and an allergy to shellfish…"

Frank made notes on the flip chart paper. "What about before his work at the clinic?"

Bailey frowned. "That looks like it'll take a bit more digging. Nothing is popping to the surface." She looked back at her father's report and then raised an eyebrow as she continued to search. "It doesn't look like my dad found much, either. How deep do you want me to go?"

Frank put up his hands. "Don't break any laws." His voice was firm. "We'll get a warrant if we need to, but, for now, stay within the databases that are accessible to the general public."

She sighed but turned back to her screen. "Okay. Here's something. He posted a CV online as part of a presentation he gave on the effects of Neupogen, a cancer drug that helps boost white blood cell numbers in people with immune deficiencies."

She scanned the screen. "Looks like the clinic where he worked was in New Jersey. He was there about four years. He published a couple of research papers during that time and did some teaching."

"What about before New Jersey?"

"Nothing yet. That's actually a bit weird. Usually I can find all kinds of stuff about someone going back to their childhood. Fredericks's life seems to have begun ten years ago when he showed up at that clinic."

"Keep digging. There has to be something."

Bailey spent another fifteen minutes digging and then shrugged her shoulders. "I'm coming up dry. There just doesn't seem to be anything before his life began in New Jersey."

"What about the stuff he has listed on his CV? It says where and when he did his undergraduate studies, right?"

"He does go back to his bachelor's degree on that document. I just can't verify what he's claiming."

Frank took a step closer so he could see the screen better. "Don't schools hoard records forever?"

"Not in this case. Either the schools no longer exist,

or they never existed in the first place." She paused. "I'll need that warrant you mentioned if you want me to go any further. Schools don't like to release information about their students these days. Still, there should be more here than I'm finding."

"Alright. I'll call and get one if we can find some probable cause that suggests we need to dig deeper. See anything else that would make him a suspect?"

Bailey met his eyes. "Do you really think one of the candidates is involved?"

Frank shrugged. "It's too early to tell. An applicant could be involved in trying to eliminate the competition, or the murders could have something to do with Gates and that contract with Nextco. Either is a good possibility." He wasn't ready to share the Balkavian angle just yet. He decided to hold that information back for now until he was sure he could trust her. The last thing he needed was for her to know too much and then go off on her own.

She kept scanning, oblivious to his woolgathering. "Well, here's something interesting. He's on the board of a company that is heavy into researching pharmaceuticals. I wonder if that's a conflict of interest."

Frank noted that on the flip chart. "That's something else to ask him about during his interview. See anything else?"

"Not so far. I'll keep looking."

Bailey typed furiously, surprised that she was actually appreciating the camaraderie she was sharing with Kennedy. If someone had told her a few days ago that she would be sleeping in his guest bedroom and he would be cooking her an omelet, she never would have thought it possible. If they had told her she would even be enjoying herself, she would have called them lies outright. It was strange that one minute he was cuffing her, and the next, they were teaming up to find a killer. Kennedy had always been her enemy—from that first time that he had arrested her for fixing grades. No matter how much she tried to avoid him, however, their paths had continued to cross over and over again during her youth. Now, after six years of absence, their lives were once again entwined and, against all odds, she was sitting here in his kitchen, chatting over the computer screen. The irony wasn't lost on her.

"Can you set it up so if you find something it sends me an alert?" he asked. "That way we can both be kept up-to-date on whatever you discover."

She winked at him. "Sure thing. What's your email address?"

He shook his head, but she could see a smile tugging at the corner of his lips. What was done was done. She might as well joke about it. At this point, there was nothing she could do to change it.

She set a few searches in motion and then glanced at him surreptitiously over the screen of her laptop. They were only six years apart in age, yet they came from very different backgrounds. Despite their history, she was beginning to have a grudging respect for him. He lived his life in an honorable way, and he didn't compromise, regardless of the consequences. That was rare in her world.

She thought back to when they were getting shot at in the car and by the beach on Jeffries's back porch. Kennedy had used his body as a shield to protect her, even though he knew she was a thief and a criminal. The night her father died, he had protected her from flying bullets and had taken her abuse without complaint during her darkest hour of grief.

She noticed his jet-black, shortly cropped hair and firm, clean-cut features. He was a good-looking man, and the thought surprised her. She had really never noticed that about him before. She liked the way his green eyes crinkled when he was concentrating, and his broad shoulders and muscular physique seemed strong enough to carry the weight of the world. She marveled how he was able to do his job and keep such a strong moral compass. Most people she knew were quick to lie or cheat when the going got tough, but not Franklin Kennedy. His job couldn't be easy. Yet he was a straight arrow.

Could they actually be friends? She wondered if such a thing were even possible. They were so different. Even if they worked together to bring down her father's killer, there was still a giant chasm between them—the money she had stolen. Now she was trying to build a bridge across that gorge, but it was built on a very shaky foundation.

Ever since she had become a Christian, the fact that she still had the stolen money had bothered her, but she hadn't decided what to do with it, so she pushed it to the back of her mind. Admittedly, a part of her defiantly wanted to hang on to it. The insurance company had already reimbursed her victim. No one was harmed. Why shouldn't she keep it? Her life had been hard. Didn't she deserve some recompense?

Deep down, she knew her justifications were weak, but the stubborn refusal to give up the money lingered. She had grown up constantly deprived, never having anything to rely on even when her situation became truly desperate. The thought of having that money as a safety cushion, to fall back on if she needed it, was powerfully tempting.

She had promised Franklin Kennedy that she would turn the money in if he let her work with him to catch her father's killer, but could she really do that? She would have agreed to just about anything to stay out of jail so she could bring her father's murderer to justice. And even though she had given him her word, she was already planning how to escape and take the money with her once this was over. She couldn't bear the thought of going back to jail, and she could live off the money she'd stashed away for a good long time.

She hated that it had come to that, though. She was finally getting her life back on track and had taken a giant step backward when she'd gotten on her computer and found that list. She had acted without thinking and was now in a big mess that once again threatened her future.

Could she live as a fugitive? It would mean leaving everything behind and living life constantly looking over her shoulder, never knowing when or how her downfall would come.

On top of that, what was the Christian thing to do?

She was still new in her faith, but it meant so much to her—she wanted so badly to live the life God wanted for her. What if she gave some of the money to charity? Would that assuage her guilt?

She struggled with her conscience, and conviction made her feel uneasy and stressed. A battle waged within her, but, in the end, running seemed like the only viable choice. She hated to break her word, but she just couldn't go back to prison, despite her promise.

Surreptitiously, she opened another window on her computer and went to a site that was unknown to most. She needed a new identity at a minimum if she wanted to work anywhere in the US, and a new passport as well, if she ended up being forced to run across a border to escape. It paid to be prepared for anything, and getting quality documents took time. It also wasn't cheap and would probably clean out her legitimate savings. She started the process and uploaded some passport-type photos that she had stored on her laptop, and then she quickly closed the window.

She looked again at Kennedy, who was making a few more notes on the wall from the reports her father had completed. She could already imagine the disappointment in his eyes when he discovered that she had run. Now all she had to do was figure out why his opinion of her mattered.

TEN

Frank awoke with a start. He'd been dreaming… He suddenly sat up and wiped the sweat from his brow. He'd been dreaming about Bailey Cox. She had been on a train pulling out of the station, waving at him, and he had been running up the platform, trying to catch her before she escaped. There had been a knowing smile on her face, as if she were home free and there was not a thing he could do about it.

He rolled out of bed and started padding toward the guest bedroom, fighting against a sense of panic. Had the dream been a premonition? Had she run?

He knocked on the guest bedroom door, and when he got no response he opened it quickly and scanned the room. The bed was made and there was no sign of Bailey. He called himself a fool a hundred different times as he quickly headed into the living room. Her freedom and a fortune were at stake. Of course she had disappeared. Why had he trusted her to stay? What a ridiculous thing to do!

"Good morning. Want a cup of coffee?" The soft

feminine voice stopped him in his tracks and his head snapped in her direction. She was lying on his couch, her computer in her lap, and she was typing, her long slender fingers dancing above the keyboard. A steaming cup of coffee was sitting on a coaster on the coffee table by her elbow. She motioned toward the kitchen, oblivious to his distress. "I hope you don't mind, but I borrowed your coffeemaker. I was dying for some caffeine. There's still enough left for you to have a cup if you're interested."

"That's fine," he muttered, wiping the sleep from his eyes. He felt a bit silly. This was the second time he'd jumped to conclusions, assuming the worst when it came to Bailey. It wasn't fair to her, and yet he knew that trust would be a long time in coming. He couldn't erase their history, or her recent actions, from his memory. He couldn't erase his own past either or the scars that still lingered from hurts that went all the way back to his childhood. He pushed those thoughts aside. If nothing else, his dream was a reminder to stay vigilant and on his guard around Bailey.

He walked to his kitchen, found himself a mug and then poured himself some coffee and added a spoonful of sugar. It felt weird to be walking around in front of Bailey Cox wearing only a T-shirt and lounge pants, but he was caffeine-deprived himself and his clothing was way down on his priority list. This was his home, and he wanted to be comfortable here. He returned to the living room, sat down in his recliner and studied his guest. She had already taken a shower and her long brown hair was still wet and pulled back into a ponytail that she had braided down her back. Her appearance was fresh and clean. Her skin was glowing, despite the lack of makeup, and she had new blue nail polish on her nails that matched her eyes. She smelled good too. Was that lilacs? He wasn't an expert on flower scents, but whatever it was, he liked it. He pushed his thoughts back to the case. "So have you found anything?"

"Yeah, I found something really interesting. Remember our friend the CEO at the hospital, Dr. Petrela?"

"Sure."

"Well, looking at Fredericks's background, or lack of it, got me to thinking about Petrela. He said he got his doctorate from Mirianka University in Balkavia. Don't you think that's a bit weird?"

Frank sat up straighter. It was interesting that she had honed in to the Balkavian connection when he still hadn't discussed the department's Balkavian case with her. Still, he proceeded cautiously, not sure how much he was going to share with her. "Why? Granted, most doctors in the US are educated here as well, but foreign degrees aren't unheard of. What's odd about that?"

She turned and put her feet on the floor, her expression filled with excitement. "What's odd is that the university has been closed down for a few years now. And before that, it turns out, they were issuing mail-order diplomas to the highest bidder. According to my dad's report, he was having trouble verifying that the good doctor actually graduated. I wouldn't be surprised if the CEO isn't a real doctor at all. It wouldn't be the first time someone had faked their education."

Frank raised an eyebrow. "What year did they close?"

Bailey hit a few keys. "They closed about five years ago, but they were being investigated for fraud long before that."

"That's amazing." He sat up straighter and considered the implications of her discovery. "But how could he get away with it? I mean, you can't fake operating on someone. Wouldn't he have to show off his medical knowledge in his current position? Surely if he wasn't a real doctor, someone would have caught on by now."

Bailey shrugged and took a sip of her coffee. "Not necessarily. He's mostly in administration, you know, ordering supplies, drafting work schedules, that kind of thing. He's the CEO, so I doubt he even sees patients. He could get away with it for quite a while if he were careful, especially if he had a background in the sciences, which he does. At a minimum, he could talk the talk. If he had some basic medical training, he could maybe fake the rest." She put down her mug. "And if someone did seem like they were catching on to his imaginary past, changing jobs would be the best possible way to eliminate any suspicion. Out of sight, out of mind—isn't that how the saying goes? The man has definitely jumped around a lot. He claimed it was just because he discovered better opportunities, but what if he had to leave or risk exposure?"

Frank was amazed. Bailey had really hit upon something here. Was it enough of a motive for this string of crimes? Surely if the CEO was lying and his history were revealed, he would be fired immediately and humiliated, but was that enough to kill over? Maybe there was even more to the story. Maybe there would be other ramifications that would cause a man to order a murder to keep his past in the past. It was definitely worth checking out. "This is a good lead, Bailey. We can call the American Medical Association and see if he's under investigation, and the hospital, as well. If he has a motive, he might jump to the top of our suspect list. Is there any way you can verify his graduation over the internet?"

"With the school closed, I'm not sure who to contact, but I can give it a go."

"Send me the results of whatever you find."

"Sure thing." She leaned forward and he could see the enthusiasm in her eyes. "I also found something else. Check this out." She moved her computer so he could see and a video started playing in a foreign language. The screen showed a couple of men explaining how to make a small construction project of some sort. Frank moved closer so he could get a better view of the screen and hear the voices. Were they building a birdhouse?

"I don't get it. What am I looking at?"

She raised the volume. "No, don't worry about the visuals. Listen to the audio. I stumbled across this clip when I was researching the doctor's med school. The night my father was killed, the two men I heard in the alley were speaking in a foreign language. I didn't recognize it at the time, but now I'm starting to wonder if it was Balkavian. That's what these guys are speaking in the video. Do you think it sounds the same?"

Frank raised an eyebrow but focused on the men's voices. Bailey Cox was one smart cookie, and she was making real headway. Once again, he was impressed with her investigative skills and instincts. "Could be. I'm not that good at languages."

"I'm not, either," Bailey admitted, "but it wasn't one of the romance languages. It sounded Slavic. I'm no expert, but I think the audio in this clip sounds pretty similar."

Frank ran his hands through his hair. It was time to share what he knew—at least some of the details. "Bailey, we were able to discover the identity of one of the men who killed your father. His name was Adrian Bekim, and he was a Balkavian with ties to the BLU, the Balkavian Liberation Union. We're still trying to discover the identity of the other man, but your Balkavian theory has real merit. There might be something there that ties together Dr. Petrela and our BLU soldier."

She raised an eyebrow and set aside her computer. "You didn't think I should know that information about the shooter?" Her eyes instantly narrowed and sparks seemed to fly right out of them.

He put up his hands in self-defense. "Don't get angry. I don't have permission to read you into all of the details of the case."

She leaned forward, her jaw tight. "Seems a little one-sided to me. You expect me to share anything and everything I find, and since you're not willing to do the same, I just wasted twenty minutes listening to foreign videos just to discover that our perps speak Balkavian." Her hands were fisted. "You could have saved me a lot of time and trouble."

"I didn't force you to do anything, and I can't help it if we have rules about sharing information we discover during an ongoing investigation. I've been as open with you as I can."

"Oh really?" Her tone displayed her disbelief and frustration.

"Look, in the spirit of cooperation, I'll share with you that Bekim and his pal used Russian 8 mm Baikal self-defense pistols converted to fire 9 mm shells and threaded to accept a silencer. They are really popular in Europe and not something you see every day here in the States." He paused. "Of course, the serial numbers were filed off and we haven't been able to find a match in our system, so that's been a dead end so far, but we're hooking up with Interpol and hoping they can shed some more light on our Balkavian friends. Now we just have to look for a connection between them and Dr. Petrela." He put his hands down and smiled, hoping what he had revealed would abate her anger.

"You don't trust me."

It was a statement, not a question. Still, he couldn't help but respond. "I'm trying to, Bailey. But you haven't made it easy. Yesterday, I had you in cuffs, remember? And there's a history here. If you turn over the stolen money, it would go a long way toward gaining my trust."

She looked away and absently rubbed her arms. "I'm not ready to do that yet."

He shrugged. "That's your choice. For now." He stood and stretched, feeling more confident in his decision to have Bailey work with him on the case. She had come up with a good lead and, in an odd sort of way, he was proud of her and her success. It was good that they were making progress. "Let's grab some breakfast and then head out to Atlanta," he said, trying to mollify her. "I'll make some calls along the way and get the team to take a harder look at Dr. Petrela." He took another sip of his coffee and then stood. "What do you like for breakfast?"

Bailey shrugged. "Got a waffle iron?" Apparently, she had realized and accepted that trust wouldn't happen instantly and that arguing wouldn't solve anything.

"Nope."

"Pancake fixings?"

"Only if you make them from scratch."

She smiled. "I can do that. Do you actually have the ingredients?"

"Probably, but you'd have to dig for them."

She thought about that for a moment. "Fruit?"

"Grapes in the fridge." He motioned toward his room. "I'm gonna grab a shower. Make yourself at home in the kitchen and I promise to eat whatever you fix. A few snacks for the road would be appreciated too, if the mood hits you and you can find something you like."

Bailey watched him disappear down the hall, a feeling of warm satisfaction sweeping away the anger. She really couldn't blame him for his lack of trust, and he seemed sincere in giving her a chance to rise in his estimation. She still wasn't sure why his opinion mattered so much, but she knew she had pleased him with her discovery about Dr. Petrela, and the fact that she was actually contributing made her extremely happy.

She still had a lot to be thankful for. They were making progress, and nothing mattered more than finding justice for her father. It was hard to imagine that the CEO she had interviewed was a killer, but she had only been around him for a few short minutes. Bailey had learned over the years that most people only showed others what they wanted them to see. The real person underneath could be much different than the public facade. Whoever had hired those killers to eliminate her father and Mr. Jeffries hadn't just done it out of the blue. There was something much bigger going on here; she was sure of it. In fact, she was probably only beginning to scratch the surface.

She set aside her laptop and headed to the kitchen, feeling no inhibitions at all as she went through Kennedy's kitchen cabinets and searched for the ingredients she needed to make breakfast. She reminded herself that she was thankful she had a place to stay and food to eat. There were times in her life when she had had neither. Even now she was used to fending for herself. Just like Franklin Kennedy, she liked to cook and had often done so for her host when she'd been between homes. It was amazing how many times she'd been allowed to stay an extra night at a friend's house, simply because she was willing to do the cooking.

Kennedy's kitchen was immaculate and well organized, and she actually laughed out loud as she thought of how well the style and layout of the kitchen matched Kennedy's personality. She whipped up some pancake batter and melted butter in a pan on the stove, thinking of Kennedy as she did so. His beard had been scruffy when he'd emerged this morning, giving him a roguish appearance that was so different from his regular polished state that she'd almost dropped her computer in surprise. She'd never seen him totally relaxed before. This new side of him was intriguing and surprising at the same time.

She finished cooking but still didn't see any sign of Kennedy. She didn't call him for breakfast because she didn't want to rush him. Instead she grabbed her computer and quickly typed in a search for countries that didn't extradite to the United States. She needed to start planning her escape. She'd never even heard of two-thirds of the nations on the list, and the ones she did recognize she had no desire to visit, let alone live there. She examined the list further and read some descriptions. Most were Communist dictatorships. Ugh!

"Ready to eat?"

The voice startled her and she quickly hit a button on her laptop and slammed the lid down. "What?"

Kennedy raised an eyebrow. "Everything okay?"

She pushed her laptop away and took the napkin off of the plate of steaming hot pancakes, hoping her nervousness wasn't obvious. "Sure. Pancakes are ready. Hope you're hungry. I made a bunch of them."

She turned away from him, grabbed the grapes and then took a breath to calm her nerves as she rinsed them in the sink. She scowled at herself as she did so. How could she have been so stupid? Thankfully, she had her computer set to erase her history after every search, so even if Kennedy opened her computer, he wouldn't be able to find what she had been searching for. Still, that had been too close. He was good at sneaking up on her and way too good at reading her. She'd have to remember that in the future. The last thing she needed was him spying over her shoulder as she made her plans to disappear.

She turned back around and gave him a smile. He wasn't buying it. He circled the counter and stopped right in front of her. He was no longer the easygoing person she'd been talking to earlier. Now he was the consummate professional law enforcement officer. Even his clothing had changed. Now he was dressed in his normal jacket and tie, he had shaved, and, for some reason, he seemed bigger and stronger than he had before. He simply exuded authority.

"What's going on, Bailey?" He was frowning now.

"Nothing, Detective. You scared me, that's all. You know, you're really good at popping up when I don't expect you. Now let's eat before these get cold." She moved by him to carry the plate of pancakes to the table. He let her by, although she could tell that he was still suspicious.

She'd set the table earlier and now she busied herself with refreshing both of their coffees and putting the pancakes, syrup and a bowl of grapes in the middle of the table. She sat down quickly, keeping her eyes averted. She could feel his eyes on her, but she tried to act as naturally as possible as she forked two of the pancakes onto her plate. Finally, she grabbed the syrup, gathered her strength and looked up, giving him another smile as she did so. "So are you hungry or what?"

He still hadn't moved. *Please just sit down and eat*, she thought silently. She didn't need him to be questioning her further—not now when they had just started to make progress working together. He didn't answer her so she tried to change the subject. "How long does the drive to Atlanta take?"

The air felt thick. Finally, he must have made a decision, because he moved slowly to his seat and sat down, and then he grabbed a few pancakes for his own plate. "A bit over five hours. I checked the GPS a few minutes ago. Looks like that drive and interview will wipe out the entire day."

"We could just Skype him," Bailey suggested, relieved that he had moved on from her gaff.

"We could do that, but I like to see a person's body language when I interview them. It's hard to do that over Skype. I learn a lot from watching what people do as they talk." His eyes met hers and she knew he hadn't moved on after all. He didn't know what she had been looking up on her computer, but he knew it was something she didn't want him to see, and it was eating at him. She could tell by *his* expression and body language. That one small act had put the wedge back between them just when they'd seemed poised to start trusting each other. What's worse was that it was her own fault. She could have waited for a time when she knew he wouldn't be around to do her computer search, but she had pushed ahead, unconcerned about the consequences. When was she going to stop acting so impetuously?

He took a few bites but then pushed aside his plate. His focus was on something altogether different. "You know, Bailey, maybe we should make some changes to our arrangement."

A cold fear gripped her heart. All of a sudden, she wasn't too hungry, either. "Like what?" Her voice was just a tad over a whisper as she waited in trepidation. Had she totally blown this? Was he going to arrest her again, right here at his kitchen table?

His eyes seemed to be burning a hole right through her. "Like if you want to keep working together, you turn over the stolen money right now as a sign of good faith."

ELEVEN

Frank steepled his fingers, keeping his eyes on Bailey's face. She was hiding something from him, and that fact alone had totally destroyed his appetite. What had happened in the short time that he was in the shower? Just a few minutes ago, he'd felt like they were making true progress and were even acting as a team. What crazy thought had entered her brain since then that had caused her to do something that she needed to hide from him?

He knew it would be a waste of time to check the laptop. He was sure she had precautions in place. There was only one way to solve this. She needed to give up the stolen money now. Then he could trust her motives. It was the only way.

She picked up her coffee mug and took a sip, and he noticed that her hand was shaking. She had to use two hands to put the mug down without spilling it. In fact, she was acting like a frightened rabbit about to bolt.

"I can't do that," she whispered. "I can't give you the money until the case is over."

"Yes, you can. And you will." His voice brooked no argument.

She glanced at his front door a couple of times. He noticed and deliberately moved his chair so it was evident to both of them that he would block her quite effectively if she tried to run.

She finally shook her head. "If I do, then you might arrest me right now. I won't be able to continue working on the case. There's nothing to make you keep me around."

"I told you I wouldn't arrest you until we closed the case."

"But how do I know you'll keep your word if I no longer have a bargaining chip?"

"That's a chance you'll have to take. You're hiding something from me, Bailey. The deal included honesty from both of us."

Bailey shook her head. "You've already tried to change the deal once."

"For your own safety. I didn't want you in danger. I still don't, but I understand that you're willing to take those risks, and up 'til now, I've been willing to let you." He sat back, studying her, unwilling to stop pushing until he achieved his objective. "So, are you ready to tell me what you were really doing on the computer just now before I came in?" He rubbed his chin thoughtfully, trying to gentle his voice. "You know, I haven't lied to you yet. When I've had doubts, I've said so. If you can't be honest with me, though, then you're forcing me to forget about our deal right here and now and arrest you with or without the money. You were right about one thing. We have to be able to trust each other, and right now, I don't think I can trust you."

She stood and started to clear the table, but he stood as well and crossed his arms, making it clear that he was still blocking her escape and he wouldn't let the subject drop. This problem was going to be resolved now. She put the plates by the sink and then turned, both hands on the counter behind her as if she needed to hold on to something sturdy to give her the strength to speak. He noticed that her hands were still shaking. A part of him felt sorry for her, but he would not relent. This was too important.

"So, I was doing a search on the internet," she said softly.

He nodded, hopeful. "Go on."

"And I decided to see what countries don't extra-dite to the US."

He had been right. She was planning to run. A cold chill swept over him. So, his gut hadn't been wrong after all. He was relieved and disappointed at the same time. Still, he was glad she was telling him the truth. That was something, and it obviously wasn't easy for her to come clean. She had to know she was risking arrest by admitting her thoughts. Even though what she'd done was wrong, he was extremely pleased that she had opened up to him. Their relationship didn't have to be over. Maybe there was still a way to salvage this. "Did you find one you like?"

"No!" she said with a surprisingly frustrated tone. "They were almost all Communist dictatorships! Can you believe it? Who would want to live there?"

He smiled, amused at her petulance. He couldn't help himself. "Well, you gotta figure the reason why they don't have an extradition treaty with the US is because they don't have a good relationship with our government or respect our laws."

"Yeah, okay, but none of the choices even looked like a good place to *visit*."

He relaxed his arms and leaned against the counter. "So what are your plans? Bolting as soon as we make an arrest?"

She tensed. "I don't know yet. I was just considering possibilities."

Again, he could see the honesty in her face. It was a good sign. "And did you consider the fact that if you ran, I'd come after you?"

She dropped her head. "No, I didn't consider that." She paused a moment and then looked back up at him, surprise in her expression. "You wouldn't really do that, would you?"

He didn't hesitate. "Of course I would."

She suddenly took a step closer, her eyes pleading. "Okay, so I broke into your server and took a couple of emails. I admit it. But is it really that big of a deal? I mean, come on, they were just a couple of emails! They didn't contain state secrets. It wasn't a violent crime. It's not murder…"

"I don't write the laws, Bailey. You broke into a state government server, and the laws that protect them exist for a reason. Can you imagine what damage a person could do if they followed your example with worse motives? They could send policemen into dangerous situations. They could screw up vendor payments and cause businesses to go under. Patients' privacy could be breached. Thousands of innocent people could be victimized. The laws are there to protect the people. It may not seem like a big deal to you, but it is a big deal to keep the computers safe so our government is up and running properly." He paused and changed the tone of his voice. When he spoke, he instilled as much conviction as he could into his words. "It's a crime I take seriously, so if you run, I *will* find you. I'll never stop looking. You should know that up front. But I think the solution here is a simple one. Stay. Face the consequences of what you've done. If you turn over the money now, it won't be so easy for you to disappear. Let's take away the temptation. I'll contact my boss, and you can do a wire transfer from whatever bank you're using to store it."

"What makes you think I even still have the money?"

He gave another small smile. "The same way that I know you won't steal again, even if a golden opportunity presents itself. Because I know you, Bailey Cox, maybe better than you know yourself. Sure, you made the bad decision to hack our server, but you're trying to get your life in order. You have a conscience. I've checked you out, Bailey. Thoroughly. You're frugal. You worked all through your college days to pay your bills, and you don't even have a car—you take the bus everywhere. Your apartment is modest. The only thing you've ever spent any real money on is your computer, and that makes sense in your line of work. That stolen money is a burden to you, and it has been for the last six years. All this time, you haven't known what to do with it. It's been eating away at you, hasn't it? And now, all it's going to do is force you to make bad decisions. It's like a rope around your neck, just waiting to tighten." He took a step forward. "Let it go, Bailey. It's the only way to move forward and quit living in the past."

He could tell she was considering his words, but now, instead of just her hands, her whole body was shaking. He wanted to offer her comfort as she struggled with what to do, but he didn't think she would accept it from him. So he just stood there, watching her internal fight and waiting patiently for her to make her decision.

Finally, she spoke, even though she had turned away and wasn't looking at him. "I'll lose my leverage," she whispered.

"You won't need it," he said softly. He took another step closer. "I promise, on my honor, to let you work with me on this case, no matter how long it takes."

She looked up, her eyes pleading. "But what if you change your mind? What if it takes six months and your boss says you have to move on? What if you get tired of the case—of me—and want to close the file without finding the murderer? What then?"

"I won't stop," he said forcefully. "This case is important to me. Sure, I might not always be able to work on it full-time like I am now, but we'll work on it nights and weekends if we have to. I'm an honorable man, Bailey. I keep my promises, and I give you my word."

He could tell she was still battling within. It wasn't hard to understand why. As far as he knew, she'd never had anybody dependable in her entire life. But it was time for her to move forward, and he was actually hoping that she could reach down inside of herself and find the strength to trust him. He knew he was asking a lot. He also knew that, without this step, he wouldn't be able to keep working with her. Without trust, it was impossible to continue. He desperately wanted her to make the right decision.

"Trust me," he said softly, willing her to accept his words. "I won't let you down. I promise."

Bailey bit her bottom lip, feeling lost. "What you're asking…it's impossible." Her voice quavered as she spoke, and she took a step backward, trying to compose herself. She was cornered, both in his kitchen and with her decision. It had been good to tell him the truth about what she had looked up on the internet. She didn't regret it, even now. But it had put her in this mess and she honestly didn't know what to do.

Kennedy was right that disappearing would be difficult without the money at her disposal. And the money really wasn't hers. She had been feeling more and more convicted every time she considered spending a dime of it. And Kennedy was also right that she wouldn't be stealing again. But could she give up her security blanket? Would Kennedy really do what he said? She considered what she knew about the man standing before her.

He was good at his job—focused and determined. He'd proven that when he first arrested her back in high school. She'd always thought his motivation was just to enforce the law and put her in jail, but now that she was spending a bit more time with Franklin Kennedy, she was starting to understand there was a lot more to this man than just the uniform. Even now, he was here, pushing for her to make the right decisions and face the consequences of her actions. He wasn't gratified when she did the wrong thing. He truly wanted her to be successful and learn from her mistakes.

His voice broke into her thoughts. "No, it's not impossible. You can do this. I know you can." His tone was gentle now and almost her undoing.

Maybe he would compromise. Then they could both be happy with the outcome. "How about I give you half now, half later?" she offered. "I can…"

"All of it, Bailey. It has to be all of it. Today. Right here. Right now." His voice was firm.

She looked up and met his eyes, expecting to see condemnation and reproach. Instead, his eyes were filled with hope—hope and confidence that she would do the right thing. She was scared, but she realized she believed Franklin Kennedy when he said he would keep working the case and let her help. He *was* an honorable man. Still, it was hard for her to trust anyone. She had been burned enough times to have learned that lesson well.

She felt as if someone were gripping her heart and making it difficult for her to breathe. Could she do it? Did she have the strength?

Finally, she made her decision. She glanced around the room until she saw a small notepad and pencil by a cell phone–charging station on the counter. She exhaled heavily and grabbed a pencil. When she was done writing, she handed Kennedy the paper. It was the hardest thing she'd ever done.

"Okay. You win, Kennedy. Here's the bank account

information and password for my Cayman account. If you give this to your boss, he should be able to transfer the money to wherever it goes. It's all there except about $40,000 that I used to pay my mother's hospital bills. You can check the amount with the hospital."

Kennedy smiled. He took her hand with the note and held it gently, and then he slowly removed the paper and put it in his pocket. "*You* win, Bailey. You made the right decision. I won't let you down. I promise."

Dear God, please let this be the right thing to do, she prayed silently. She didn't know how this would all turn out, but she did know one thing—despite the fear, she felt as if a giant weight had just been removed from her shoulders. She was thankful for that.

TWELVE

Bailey paced a bit, waiting for Kennedy to get off the phone. He had wasted no time calling his boss with the bank information and was still in the bedroom, discussing the situation with him. Nervousness tied a knot in her stomach. Would Kennedy arrest her when he finished his call? She believed he'd try to keep his word...but it wasn't really his decision, was it? His boss had final say.

Should she grab her things and disappear out the door before he returned? She had no plan and now no money. What should she do? Nervousness fluttered within her. He wanted her trust, but she really didn't know how to give him that.

His bedroom door suddenly opened and she took a step backward and then another as he emerged. The closer he got, the further she withdrew. Finally, he figured out what was going on and stood still in the middle of his living room.

"Bailey, are you okay?"

"Are you going to arrest me now?" she blurted out, unable to control her anxiety.

"No, Bailey. I told you I wouldn't." His voice was patient, relaxed. "In fact, I just gave the bank information to my boss and he gave me some good news. He said that since you volunteered the information, he would talk to the DA about you hacking our email server and try to get you a lighter sentence through a plea agreement. He said we could keep working together on this case and was impressed with the extra info you provided on the Balkavian angle. Officially, you're now a consultant, which means we can share more than we have been." He smiled at her. He actually had a nice smile, and for a moment she was lost in thought, trying to remember if and when he had ever smiled at her like that before. When he was smiling, he seemed approachable, even friendly.

"Are you ready to go?"

His words broke through her woolgathering and she startled. "Where are we going?" She was so worried that it was hard to even process what he was saying. Had he already changed his mind about taking her to jail?

"Atlanta, remember? We have an interview with the doctor scheduled for 3:30 this afternoon. We need to leave now if we're going to make it on time. Are you ready?"

She gave herself a mental shake. "Yeah, I just need to grab my computer." She skirted around him, picked up her laptop and then grabbed her tote bag from the couch. He seemed to understand her uneasiness and didn't react when she avoided getting close to him. He even seemed to be moving more slowly so as not to scare her. He was scoring big points in the being-understanding category. She tried to push the thought of more years behind bars to the back of her mind and concentrate on the here and now. Right now, the only thing that mattered was getting justice for her father.

"Should we take the grapes for a snack?" he asked over his shoulder as he headed to the kitchen. He pulled a small cooler from the top of the fridge and grabbed an ice pack from the freezer. "How about some soda, as well?"

"Yes to both. What kind of soda do you have?"

"Root beer? Dr. Pepper? What's your pleasure?"

Bailey shrugged. "Whatever you pick is fine." His nonchalant attitude was helping her relax and again she appreciated his efforts. She watched him as he stowed the grapes and soda and then added a bag of pretzels to the top. Their relationship was tentative, at best. Trust was a difficult thing for her to give… Could she do it?

He opened the door and allowed her to leave before him. Then he turned and locked his apartment and joined her on the stairs for the descent, jingling his car keys as he did so. "What kind of music do you like?" he asked, keeping his voice low and nonthreatening.

"Christian pop is what I listen to the most," she answered. "How about you?"

"I'm a country fan, I must admit, but I like Christian pop too. I can live with that once we hit the road. I think I even have a few CDs in the car that you might like."

"CDs? No iPod?"

He laughed. "I'm old-school."

A few minutes later, they were on the road with Steven Curtis Chapman serenading them via the stereo.

Neither of them had seen any cars tailing them, but, every so often, each checked the rearview mirrors, just in case. The first hour, Bailey was still so uptight she could barely sit still, but, as the miles flew by, she slowly started to relax and, by the fourth hour, they were talking pretty easily. She realized she really didn't know much about this man beside her, and she figured maybe it was time she learned more, especially if they were going to keep working together, as he'd promised.

"So, you've researched my life and know everything about me. Right?"

Kennedy laughed. "Well, I wouldn't say I know *everything* but, yes, I've learned a great deal." He took the time to look at her for a moment and then turned his eyes back to the road. "I'm really impressed by your investigation skills. Not just with computers, but overall. You're smart and have good intuition. That kind of info isn't available in a background check."

The compliment surprised her, but she wasn't quite sure how to receive it. She wasn't used to receiving compliments, especially from him, and they made her feel awkward. She pushed forward. "So we're a little uneven, don't you think? I mean, all I know about you is that you're good at your job and you like to fish."

"You also know I like root beer and Steven Curtis Chapman's music."

"You're right. I'll add those to the list."

He smiled. He really did have a killer smile. And she liked it when his green eyes were bright and approachable, as they were now. "So what would you like me to tell you about?"

"Everything. Start at the beginning. I mean, we have another hour to kill, right?"

He raised an eyebrow. "I certainly don't want to bore you for an hour." There was mirth in his voice.

Wow. That had come out totally wrong. She tried again. "No, I didn't mean it like that. I mean we have plenty of time so you can tell me the details. I really do want to know." That surprised her, but the more she thought about it, the more she realized she wasn't just being polite. She truly wanted to understand what made this man tick. Over the last few days he had become a very important person in her life.

He pursed his lips as if unsure where to start, so she helped him out. "Are you from Jacksonville?"

"No, but I grew up just south of here in Palm Bay. Then I went to college at Florida State. Go Seminoles!"

"Ah, so you must be a football fan."

He made the usual chopping gesture always seen at Seminoles games. "Football, track, soccer, baseball—even basketball. I love them all. I don't watch much pro, but I enjoy the college rivalries."

"Did you ever play yourself?"

"A little football in high school, but I wasn't good enough to make it at the college level. The sheriff's office has a couple of softball teams, and I play with them to stay in shape. It's a lot of fun. We play against other units across the city and sometimes against the firefighters, that sort of thing."

Bailey was silent for a minute and Kennedy finally looked over at her to see what was going on.

"So, I already bored you, didn't I? I knew it would happen. I'm not a very flashy guy."

Bailey shook her head. "I'm not bored at all. It's just I'm having a hard time picturing you relaxing enough to play sports. You're pretty intense."

He frowned. "Is that a bad thing?"

"Not necessarily. It's what makes you so good at your job."

"Well, my job is important to me. It's who I am."

"It's who you are when you're on the clock. Who are you the rest of the time?"

Kennedy paused for a moment. "I guess I don't see it like that. I'm a cop all of the time. Sure, I'm off duty sometimes, but I never take off the blue."

"Is that why you're not married?"

Kennedy whistled. "Boy, you don't pull any punches, do you?"

Bailey smiled. "I guess I never was any good at subtlety. So? What's the answer?"

"I've dated here and there," Kennedy finally answered, "but being married to a cop isn't an easy life, and so far I haven't found anyone who wanted to go the distance." He turned again and raised his eyebrows. "Okay, your turn. Why haven't you tied the knot?"

Bailey shrugged. "I've never been in love before." She absently pulled some lint off her shirt, thinking back through her life. "I've had some friends over the years, but nobody really special."

"Do you ever let anybody get close?"

Bailey met his eye. The accuracy with which he had just hit the bull's-eye made her a little uncomfortable, but she answered with honesty. "Not really. I guess I'm pretty good at pushing people away. I'm scared, you know, that if I let somebody in and they end up hurting me, I won't survive it."

Kennedy nodded. Since he did know her history, he actually might understand where she was coming from.

"You're tougher than you think." His voice was gentle and somewhat comforting, as well. He could be really nice when he wanted to be. She liked that.

"Thanks." She looked out the window for a moment and then turned back to him again. "So, is that something you want? You know, a wife, kids, the white picket fence?"

He didn't hesitate. "Yes, when the right person comes along. How about you?"

"I'd like that, but I don't really think that's in my future."

Kennedy seemed surprised by her answer. "Really? Why not?"

"Well, I don't have much of a future to look forward to, and, really, who would want someone like me with my past? I mean, get real—I've been in prison. That kinda limits the options, you know?"

He took her hand and squeezed it, and then he didn't let go right away like she expected. She wasn't used to people touching her, and her first inclination was to pull away, but she decided after a moment or two that she actually liked the contact. It made her feel safe.

"That won't matter to the right guy," he reassured her. "God has someone in mind for you. What does it say in Psalms 37? 'Delight yourself in the Lord and He will grant the desires of your heart.' To me, that means that if it's His will for your life and you are living for Him, then He'll bring the right person along."

She wasn't convinced, but it was sweet of him to say so. Yes, she believed God could do anything, but she doubted He was concerned about something as insignificant as her loneliness.

It was time to change the subject to something else—something that didn't remind her of the prison sentence looming in front of her because of her thoughtless, impetuous act.

"Do you have brothers? Sisters?"

"I have a sister who lives in Washington, DC. She's in law school at Georgetown."

"Smart girl."

Kennedy laughed. "Yeah, she's the one who has all the brains in the family."

Bailey joined him in the laugh. "Yeah, right."

Frank enjoyed her laugh. He glanced down at their joined hands and found himself enjoying the touch, as well. Taking her hand has been a spur-of-the-moment idea because he'd wanted to comfort her, but now he found himself appreciating the contact more than he expected. He wanted to draw his thumb over the back of her hand, but he refrained, afraid that he would scare her off. She was still acting like a frightened rabbit, and she was hesitant to receive compliments, let alone physical touch.

Their conversation and her skittishness made him wonder about her childhood and the disparity of their lives. He had been raised with love and support. She had obviously had to fend for herself, and while that had made her tough and resilient, it also made for a solitary existence. She was obviously a product of her environment, and it was amazing that she had turned out as well as she had.

The lady beside him had overcome terrific odds and still gotten her college degree. And, he reminded himself, she had worked the entire time, rather than depending upon the ill-gotten gains from her crime to meet her expenses. That must have taken a great deal of fortitude to accomplish. She had worked so hard to rise above her beginnings—was it truly the right thing to push her back into jail and wreck her future?

Frank was beginning to realize that the law might have room for some shades of gray. That thought gave him pause. He had always seen things in black and white. If you broke the law, you went to jail. It was simple. It was clean. But maybe there was a messiness involved that needed consideration.

And speaking of shades of gray... He glanced out the back of his window, noticing the silver sedan that had been a few cars behind them for the last ten miles or so. He sped up a bit and changed lanes, and, once again, the silver car kept pace with him. He glanced at his GPS and followed the directions to exit at the next ramp. They had entered the city limits some time ago and were almost at their destination. The silver sedan followed them.

"Do you know anyone that drives a silver Camry?"

"No." She turned to look behind them, her face full

of anxiety. "The car doesn't look familiar. Can you see the driver?"

"Not really, but my guess is it's another one of our Balkavian friends. He's wearing a navy baseball cap and aviator sunglasses. I got the first three letters of his license plate." Frank called his contact in the Atlanta Police Department and updated her about the Camry, staying on the phone with her even as sirens approached. He had been assured full cooperation from the local police, and was thankful for the assistance. The silver car kept pace for another minute or so and then fell back and exited with the police following him. Frank kept driving, exiting at the next opportunity. According to the GPS, they were only two blocks away from their destination.

"Wow, what's all this?" Bailey asked as she noticed the heavy street congestion and blue lights reflecting off of the buildings up ahead.

"It looks like the police are involved with something at the building where our doctor works. Let's park and investigate. And keep your eye open for that silver car and the driver as we go."

It took a while to find parking, and by the time they had walked back on the sidewalk to the edge of the crime tape, Frank's phone rang. "Looks like the silver car has disappeared," he told Bailey after hanging up. "They chased him for about ten miles and lost him. He's probably long gone, but stay alert in case he circles back."

"You got it."

Frank noted the address on the building that was cordoned off and checked it against his notes. It was definitely the doctor's building, and several policemen were walking about, interviewing people on the street, taking notes and talking amongst themselves. He walked up to one of them and flashed his badge.

"Hi, I'm Franklin Kennedy from the Jacksonville sheriff's office. We've got an appointment in this building with Dr. Fredericks at 3:30 this afternoon. He's a person of interest in a case we're working. Sergeant Adams is my APD contact. Can you tell me what's going on?"

"I think your appointment will have to be postponed," the policeman said grimly. "Someone just tried to kill Dr. Fredericks. They took two shots at him through his office window."

THIRTEEN

"Is he alive?" Kennedy asked, his hands on his hips.

"Yes, he wasn't injured, but he's been escorted down to the station to be interviewed."

Kennedy clipped his badge to his belt so it was clearly visible. "Can we take a peek at the crime scene?"

The policeman lifted the yellow tape so the two of them could pass to the other side. "You'll have to square it with the OIC." The policeman answered as he pointed to the officer in charge, who was standing by a group of officers near the building entrance.

Kennedy nodded his thanks and motioned for Bailey to keep quiet and follow him. Fortunately, the OIC was friendly, and once Kennedy explained why they were there and the connection between the cases, the OIC cleared them both to go upstairs and check out the crime scene.

"You usually get such good cooperation?" Bailey asked, a little surprised. She'd always thought there was more antagonism between law enforcement agencies, but she was pleasantly surprised by the Atlanta policeman's helpful attitude.

"Not always, but we're on the same side. A lot of officers understand that. The wall of blue is pretty powerful."

"Evidently," Bailey agreed. They rode the elevator to the fifth floor and easily found the office where the shooting had occurred. Kennedy again talked to the local police and explained their presence while Bailey scanned the room. There actually wasn't too much to see. Two bullet holes were clearly visible in the glass wall facing the street, but the glass hadn't shattered. Instead the bullets had left circles of damaged glass about three inches wide around the holes. The holes were about five feet from the floor near a large potted palm. She turned toward the desk. Across the room, crime techs had marked where they'd found the bullets embedded in the bookcase. She guessed that the killer had probably been aiming at Dr. Fredericks working at his desk. Apparently, the perpetrator has missed both times.

"Any leads on the shooter?"

Bailey turned her attention back to Kennedy and the conversation he was having with the Atlanta detective. The man shook his head in response to Kennedy's question.

"Nope. We've found the probable apartment the shooter used due to the angle, but there was no brass or other clues left behind."

"What about the bullets?" Kennedy asked.

"They look like .39 rounds, which is a bit weird."

"That's standard ammunition for the AK-47, right?"

The detective nodded. "Yep, as well as a few other models like the Soviet SKS. We just don't see that very often. Usually, for a job like this, the perp would use a Remington 700 with a .30-06 bullet."

Bailey found that interesting and filed it away for later research. If she remembered correctly, the use of an AK-47 was another tie to Balkavia. She thought she remembered seeing somewhere that the Russian-made rifle was a Balkavian favorite. The evidence against Dr. Petrela was getting stronger, although even she had to admit that it was still all circumstantial at this point. They hadn't found any proof yet that he was guilty of anything.

She watched Kennedy out of the corner of her eye, impressed with both the questions he was asking and the way he carried himself. He was a professional, through and through. She'd always known that, but in the past she had been so convinced he was the enemy that she had never really slowed down to watch him do his job and see the way he related to people and made them feel at ease.

Kennedy finished up his conversation and started walking around the room. Bailey followed him, looking for anything out of the ordinary. There were a couple of other bookcases filled with medical texts but no personal photos or other mementos, and the pictures on the walls were abstract art that also revealed little about the doctor who worked here. She looked at the bullet holes and glanced across the street at the other building where the shooter must have been. It was a nondescript apartment building. Her gaze swung back to the bullet holes and the cracks in the glass and then went down to the carpet. There were tiny bits of glass embedded in the light-colored fiber, as well as a dark water stain about the size of her fist.

The stain looked old and, if she had to guess, she figured someone, sometime, had overwatered the palm and caused the damage. She imagined the plant itself usually covered the stain, but it had been moved aside. To allow the investigators to examine the glass? Or... perhaps for some other reason?

The funny thing about bullets entering through this type of glass was that there was no way to say when they had been fired. She wondered if Dr. Fredericks was telling the truth about when this all occurred. It was almost as if the assault had happened previously but had been kept hidden behind the plant. Then the doctor had waited to report it until it fit his time schedule, at which point he had moved the plant to reveal the damaged pane.

She shook her head, trying to wash away the conspiracy theories floating around in her head. Dr. Fredericks was a victim. Plain and simple. She had no right to prejudge him and look for sinister motives. But she wouldn't fully dismiss the ideas, either. She'd get a better read on him when they interviewed him, but for now she kept her mouth shut.

There was not much else to see. Kennedy turned. "Anything else you want to take a peek at?"

Bailey shook her head. "No, but I'm ready to talk to the doctor."

"We should be able to get in to see him. The OIC gave me directions to the precinct where he's holed up. Ready to go?"

"Sure thing." She followed him out, her mind filled with questions. "Do you think Dr. Petrela really believes that killing all of the other applicants will ensure he gets offered the position?"

"Well, somebody sure is trying to eliminate them. The motive you discovered is plausible, but we have to consider other possibilities, as well. Let's see if Dr. Fredericks has any more answers that can help us piece this thing together."

It didn't take them long to reach the police precinct or for Frank to ease their way in to see the doctor. David Fredericks was shorter than Frank expected, and had dark hair and eyes that reminded him of an old Italian buddy from his college days. Fredericks's eyes were not nearly as friendly, however, and even though he smiled and shook both their hands during the introduction, there was something off about the doctor that bothered him. Call it gut instinct. Call it experience. Frank couldn't put his finger on the problem, but he could see that the doctor was assessing them just as carefully as Frank was evaluating him.

So far, he'd noted that Fredericks was surprisingly cool and collected, which Frank thought seemed a bit odd since he had just been the victim of attempted murder. In fact, Frank knew that his own office had notified the doctor about Cox's and Gabriel Jeffries's murders, as well. Wasn't he the least concerned that his life was in danger? Either he was missing something or the doctor had ice in his veins.

Frank glanced around the small room, furnished with

a table and four chairs. He sat in one, motioning for Bailey to sit next to him and for Dr. Fredericks to sit across from them. "I'm sorry about what happened, Dr. Fredericks. I know you've already been through the story with the local police, but if you wouldn't mind, I'd like to hear your version of the events."

Fredericks sat and rubbed his beard thoughtfully. Frank was struck by both the man's manicured hands and his well-groomed appearance. Not a hair was out of place, despite the episode this afternoon. He put that fact in the *odd* category, as well.

"Well, there isn't all that much to tell," Fredericks intoned. "I was sitting at my desk, going over some files, when I accidentally dropped some loose papers. As I bent over to pick them up, I heard a faint popping sound. I really didn't know what to make of it until I saw the holes in the books behind me. I instantly dropped to the floor and called 911 with my cell phone, and the police responded within minutes. I was still waiting on the floor when they arrived." He cleared his throat and crossed his legs. "I understand that they weren't able to catch the person who did this."

Frank made a few notes on his iPad and then looked up. "Not yet." He typed a bit more and then he leaned forward. "But it's only a matter of time." He set the iPad on the table. "Do you mind if we go over the reason for our appointment today? I know you're probably still in shock from your experience, but I believe the two cases might be related, and I'd like to ask you a few questions."

Fredericks leaned back. "I don't mind at all. Please, ask your questions."

Again, Frank was surprised about the man's carefree and cocky attitude. People handled stress in different ways—he knew that. But the doctor's mannerisms made his flesh crawl. He always wanted to remain objective when dealing with a victim or a suspect, but his dislike of Dr. Fredericks hit him strongly, and it was hard to overcome. Hard but not impossible. Frank pushed forward and told him the basics about Cox's death, Gates and what had happened at Gabriel Jeffries's beach house, just in case there had been a miscommunication leaving the man unaware of the danger the applicants were facing.

Fredericks reacted with shock at the mention of the dead CEO at the beach; however, his behavior seemed almost over-the-top and rehearsed. "Then this afternoon's shooting was only the beginning. It sounds like I'm still in danger."

Frank nodded. "It's a definite possibility. Tell me about why you want the Gates job?"

"Honestly, I'm tired of dealing with patients," Dr. Fredericks stated without pretense. "I'll be the first to admit my bedside manner is lacking. Any joy I ever felt at dealing with the general populace has completely disappeared. Running Gates seemed like the next logical step in my career given my medical background and skill set. I'm anxious to get behind the wheel of that company and drive it into the future."

Frank made a few notes. "We do background checks on all of the people of interest in a case. It's standard procedure. With you, though, we've had a little trouble. Can you tell us where you were about ten years ago and what you were doing?"

Fredericks coughed. "It's all in my CV. I ran a clinic in New Jersey. I'll have my assistant send over the document."

Frank nodded as if he didn't already have a copy. "What about before the clinic?"

"Like I said, it's all in the CV. Today has been rather harrowing and I can't even think straight right now. I'll be happy to look through my records and send you whatever supporting documents you need tomorrow."

Frank took more notes, aware that the man was now dodging his questions. "That would be fine." He handed the man his business card and Fredericks pocketed it.

"Do you have any enemies in your past—disgruntled colleagues, angry patients, maybe personal problems— that could explain the attack on you today?"

Fredericks sputtered, looking genuinely thrown for a minute before his mask slipped back into place. "Isn't it obvious that this happened because I'm Gates's top choice? The perpetrator must be one of the other applicants who's trying to eliminate the competition. Have you checked them all out?"

"We're doing that now," Frank answered. "In fact, that's one reason why we came here today. Have you heard anything from Gates to make you believe they have changed their hiring plans?"

"I have an appointment with Mr. Johnson later this week, but with this new set of events, I'm not sure what to think. I'll have to give him a call and see where things stand. I don't want this unpleasantness to alter their timeline."

"Unpleasantness?" Frank raised an eyebrow. What a callous way to refer to the deaths of two men.

"Naturally, I mean today's shooting. Once you bring the culprit to justice, Gates won't have to worry about hiring extra security for me, that sort of thing."

"Aren't you on the board of a company that does pharmaceutical research?" Bailey piped up.

Fredericks's eyes fluttered to Bailey but then returned to Frank as if he dismissed her importance. "I am, but their research focuses specifically on cancer treatment drugs. There is no conflict between my work with that firm and the position at Gates. Gates doesn't handle cancer drugs."

"How familiar are you with Gates's recent products?" Frank asked.

"Well, I did my research before applying for the job, if that's what you're asking. They're on the cusp of making several exciting discoveries and will be a major player in the pharmaceutical market for the foreseeable future."

"Actually, I'm just wondering if you can think of any reason why Gates could be the target of all of this violence. Maybe their business practices have caused a problem or…"

"This can't be related to anything Gates is involved in. That company is sound and a well-respected leader in the field. Otherwise, I never would have applied. I don't waste my time on people or organizations that aren't the top of the line."

"Have you ever been to Balkavia, Greece or Kosovo?" Bailey asked.

Fredericks again barely looked at her and directed his response to Frank. "No, why do you ask?"

"Just chasing down all possible leads, Dr. Fredericks," Frank responded. He stood and Bailey joined him. "Thank you for your time."

"One more quick question, Dr. Fredericks," Bailey said.

He sighed in obvious frustration but turned his attention toward her. "Yes?"

"Is it possible that the attack at your office happened at some other time, but you're just reporting it today?"

Fredericks narrowed his eyes. "Now, why would I do that?"

"Well, if *you* are the applicant who wanted the others out of the competition, then one way to avoid suspicion would be to stage a shooting so you'd look like a victim instead of a perpetrator."

The man's face turned red and Frank raised an eyebrow. He was surprised by Bailey's question, yet he still wanted to hear the doctor's answer.

Fredericks stood and turned away from Bailey, giving his full and undivided attention to Frank alone. "The shooting happened today, just as I reported it. I *am* the victim here, and I resent any implication otherwise. You will keep me informed of how the investigation progresses, won't you?" He pulled out a business card from his pocket. "You can call my secretary or answering service at any time."

Frank nodded. "Absolutely." He watched the man go and then turned to Bailey.

"What was that all about?"

Bailey shrugged. "The man is creepy. But, besides that, the plant in his office by the bullet holes looked like it had been moved to show the holes. I'm not doubting someone shot his window. I'm just wondering when it actually happened. Maybe he waited until he knew we were coming to question him, and then he staged this whole thing so we'd think he was a victim like the others, and we wouldn't look too closely into his past."

"Why didn't you say something at the scene?"

She glanced around nervously. "I wasn't sure if you'd be interested."

He put his hands on her shoulders and waited until she looked at him. "I am always interested in what you see and hear. Don't be afraid to tell me what you're thinking. Ever. Okay?" She nodded and he released her. He'd had his own doubts about Dr. Fredericks but hadn't been able to identify any holes in his story. Being creepy wasn't a crime, but he was glad to be out of the man's presence. Still, something told him he hadn't seen the last of Dr. Fredericks.

They left the room and headed back down to the car. He glanced over at Bailey, who still seemed quiet as if she was in her own world. He tried to bring a smile to her face. "Look, I know I'm way out of your league when you compare our computer skills, but aren't you going to even notice how I've started using an iPad now to take my notes instead of my old spiral notebooks?"

His banter had the desired effect and she smiled.

"Yeah, I was wondering when you were going to join the modern world. I remember I teased you quite a bit about that back in the day."

"Teased?" He raised an eyebrow. "I'd say *harassed* is more like it. You wouldn't leave me alone, always saying how I'd be left behind if I didn't catch up to technology."

They both laughed. When they'd first met, Frank had definitely been a rookie and had always carried a small black spiral notebook in his top left pocket. He'd known next to nothing about computers and still carried a flip phone.

"So have you learned anything in the past six years?"

"Oh yeah. I've learned what an app is, and I've learned how to play Trivia Crack. Are you impressed?" He held up his tablet and took her picture. "And I've learned how to take pictures with the iPad. Smile! Make sure I get your best side!"

She laughed in earnest now, covered her eyes and then pushed his hand away as he put the iPad closer for a tighter shot. "Enough! I don't look good in pictures."

"Says who?" he said as he snapped a few more. He finally stopped and stowed the iPad when she ducked behind him.

"Says me. I'm not an idiot. I've seen myself in the mirror before."

"Then you know you're beautiful."

"Yeah, right." Her voice was filled with derision.

He stopped walking and tilted his head. "You're kidding, right?"

She averted her gaze. "Why are we talking about this? Let's change the subject."

He agreed but was still surprised. Did she truly not realize how pretty she was? In his eyes, she'd always been beautiful. And now that she had matured, she carried herself with newfound confidence and grace. When he paused and thought about her history, though, he realized she'd probably had to deal with quite a bit of self-doubt over the years, leading to insecurity. That was a shame. He hoped someday someone would appreciate her. Even though she was a bit unpolished, she was still quite a gem.

Once they were in the car and on the freeway again, Frank's stomach growled so loudly that it embarrassed him. "Sorry," he said softly. "I guess skipping breakfast and lunch has made me a bit hungry. Those grapes we ate were gone hours ago."

"Look, there's a diner coming up! Let's stop there," Bailey said suddenly, pointing at a sign. A few minutes later, they were sitting at the Varsity, a fast-food drive-in restaurant that specialized in orange soda, onion rings and delicious hamburgers. The store was decorated like an old drive-in from the 1950s with black-and-white tile and red accents. The entire store was filled with an ambience of carefree fun and he noticed several carhops dancing their food to the cars parked outside. Frank was decidedly uncomfortable, but when he looked at Bailey, he could tell that she was in her element.

"It's okay to relax, Detective Kennedy," she said with a smile, obviously aware that he felt out of place.

"I'm relaxed," he said quickly but then smiled in return. He wasn't fooling her, and he knew it. "Okay, I'm a bit stiff. I get it. This place is filled with confusion, and that's something I tend to avoid."

"Fun can be organized or spontaneous." She leaned forward, grabbed a paper forage hat from a stack on the counter and put it on his head. "Now you fit in!"

His first instinct was to quickly remove the hat to avoid looking ridiculous, but he knew rejecting her gesture would bother her. He'd already pushed her rather hard today, and he didn't want to stomp on her feelings. After all, she'd surrendered the money and left herself vulnerable to him. And, good grief, it was just a hat. Was he really that uptight? "Now I look like I belong behind the counter." He tried to smile, but he just felt silly, so it was hard to do.

"It's okay to be silly too," she said with a grin.

"So now you're reading my thoughts?"

"Look, I know you're a straight arrow, but sometimes you have to live a little."

He shrugged. "I'm not sure this is what you should call *living*."

She offered him an onion ring. "Try this, and then decide."

He wasn't sure if it was because he was so hungry or if the food was really that good, but the next thing he knew he was finishing off the basket of onion rings and heading back to buy another. "Okay, you win. This food is fantastic. I guess I can wear the hat in public if I get these onion rings as the prize."

She laughed and he felt himself laughing with her. It felt good. In fact, he realized he hadn't laughed this much in a very long time. He hadn't smiled much, either. His job was filled with serious issues and problems, yet Bailey had shown him that it actually felt good to relax a bit and enjoy the moment.

All of this time, he thought he'd been the one trying to teach Bailey how to make wise decisions, but maybe he could learn something from her too. Maybe he did need to enjoy life a bit more. He ate another onion ring, enjoying both the company and the food immensely.

FOURTEEN

Frank saw no sign of the silver sedan or any other tail on their way home, but he continued to keep an eye out until they had parked outside his apartment building. Bailey had slept most of the trip, and he'd spent most of the time on the phone with Detective Ben Graham as they discussed the case. He turned off the motor and then turned to Bailey, who had just woken up and was stretching with a yawn.

"Welcome back."

She yawned again. "Wow, I guess I needed that nap. How long was I out?"

"About two hours. I've got a lot to tell you. Ben just gave me some updates." He started to get out, but Bailey put her hand on his arm and stopped him.

"Are you sure I need to keep imposing on you? I can go back to my apartment…"

"No, I want you here," he answered quickly.

"I'm not going to disappear on you. I promise. I'm going to see this case through to the end. I want to know who's responsible for my father's death, and I'm not going to quit until I get an answer."

Frank reached over and squeezed her hand. "I believe you, but I'm still worried about your safety. You've been knocked out and shot at, and your father's death only happened a couple of days ago. I don't think it's good for you to be alone." He paused. "Besides, it's really no imposition, and it's helpful to have you here to go over the details of the case."

She finally gave in, but he could still see the hesitance in her eyes. The camaraderie they'd shared at the restaurant had lessened and she seemed withdrawn again. He sighed inwardly. He didn't want her to feel uncomfortable in his presence. In fact, now that the money no longer stood between them and his boss had committed to working out a deal for her email hacking, he'd hoped that she would feel even more comfortable working together. He chose to confront the issue, rather than ignore it.

"So? What are you thinking?"

"Nothing."

"Nothing?"

She squeezed his hand back and released it. "Nothing. I guess I'm just still trying to figure things out. Today was a big day for me, and I feel kind of lost." She moved to get out of the car, and he let her, sensing that she needed some space. He wanted to offer her support, but he also wanted to give her time to work through the changes without smothering her.

As much as he wanted to review the updates with her, he felt it was time for a break from all the chaos and tragedy. They would have plenty of time tomorrow to go over his notes and plan their next move.

A new thought hit him. Was she still planning to run, even though she'd given up the stolen money? He believed her when she said she'd stay through the end of the case, but then what? Even though his boss had promised leniency, he hadn't promised a free pass. Bailey was still looking at prison time, and it had to be weighing heavily on her, on top of everything else.

He grimaced and then followed her up the stairs to his apartment. Even when Bailey was quiet, her body language spoke volumes. Right now, he needed to wait and watch.

The baby wouldn't quit crying, no matter how much the young mother bounced the little girl on her knee. The child playing next to her must not have liked the noise, because the next thing Frank knew, the little boy was bawling too. Somebody also needed a diaper change, according to his nose.

"Dr. Merritt is ready to see you," the receptionist said with a smile, apparently oblivious to the noise. Maybe she could tune it out, but he wasn't able to, and he was more than ready to interview the fourth applicant for the Gates CEO position and get out of the waiting room full of sick and crying children.

Bailey was right beside him, as usual, and followed him into the doctor's office. The rest of the evening after their trip had been uneventful, and this morning Bailey had awoken fresh and ready to hit the ground running. Over breakfast, Frank had caught her up on all of the evidence his unit had discovered, the most important being that they had finally identified the second shooter from her father's murder.

They now knew that both men were Balkavian mercenaries with ties to the BLU and the war in Balkavia. They also had a history of crime in both Europe and the US, and Interpol was helping the Jacksonville unit track down some of their known associates on the Eastern Seaboard. The investigation was growing into a much larger case than they had anticipated, and even the FBI had been called in.

Meanwhile, Frank was still concerned about the silver sedan that he'd seen yesterday, and a black truck appeared to be following them today. At least no one was taking shots at them...yet. The possibilities kept his senses on high alert, but nothing kept him more vigilant than Bailey Cox.

Bailey was different today, and the worry she had displayed the night before seemed to have disappeared. Now that the money wasn't an issue between them, Frank found himself noticing even more positive things about her, like the way her smile lit up her face as she warmed herself with her coffee and the way her hair framed her face perfectly.

They had talked and even laughed during breakfast and the drive here, and he'd found himself sharing stories from his childhood that he'd never told anyone before. She had also opened up and told him a bit about her time in college and the fun she'd had in her computer classes. He found her vivacious personality endearing, and the more he knew, the more he liked. It was an odd feeling for him to acknowledge.

He had been so focused on catching criminals that he hadn't really spent any time on a social life. He had told her that he played softball and cooked for fun, but when he sat down and thought about it, he realized he rarely spent time even on those activities. His eighteen-hour days were filled with catching criminals and investigating, not enjoying his hobbies or spending time with friends. Bailey's presence was making him realize how big of a hole in his life there actually was.

"I'm so sorry to hear about your father," Dr. Merritt said to Bailey after the introductions were made. "No job is worth a person's life. I sure hope the Gates CEO position isn't the cause of all of this violence."

"Thank you," Bailey answered. "I appreciate your kind words."

Dr. Merritt's evident compassion was a night-and-day difference from the behavior they'd witnessed in Atlanta. Noting the contrast, Frank wondered what type of personality Gates was actually looking for in their hunt for a leader and made a mental note to dig further into the company this evening.

"We're so glad you were able to fit us into your busy schedule," Frank said with a smile. "Can you tell us why you're interested in leading Gates?"

"Well, I'll miss the kids from the office," she said with a frown, "but Gates is doing some amazing work with cancer drugs, and that has been a focus of mine within our practice. I've always had a desire to work in oncology, but lately I've been wanting to go beyond my practice and enter the business side of medicine. I want to direct the research and the focus of the industry. Gates seemed like a perfect fit."

Bailey raised an eyebrow and looked pointedly at Frank. She obviously also remembered Dr. Fredericks's comment that Gates had nothing to do with cancer pharmaceuticals. He made another note in his iPad to research that issue. "Have you met the other candidates?"

Dr. Merritt shook her head. "No. I've heard of Dr. Petrela from the hospital and know he applied, but everything else I've learned about this case I heard either from your detective who called or the newspaper. I heard there were also a couple of stories in the evening news, but I missed them both."

"What can you tell us about Dr. Petrela?" Bailey asked.

Dr. Merritt shrugged. "He's more of an office man from what I've been told and doesn't spend a lot of time actually working with patients, but that's really all I know."

"Can you think of any reason why the Gates applicants would be targeted?"

"I have no idea. It's an important job, but, like I said before, it certainly isn't worth dying over. There are other companies out there doing competitive work."

"Have you seen anything suspicious?" Frank asked. "Anything that would make you fear for your safety?"

"Not really. I've definitely been more vigilant since your detective called, and at one point I thought I was being followed, but that was two days ago, and I haven't noticed anything else since. It could have just been my imagination."

"What made you think you were being followed?"

"When I was driving in to work, a black truck seemed to be behind me all the way from my house to the office."

"Could you see the driver?"

"No. There was only one person in the vehicle, but that's about all I noticed. I couldn't even tell what type of truck it was beyond the color. It pulled away as I turned into my parking garage, and I haven't seen the truck since—or at least I haven't noticed it."

Frank stewed on this while Bailey asked a question. "Have you ever been to Balkavia or other countries in that region?"

"No. I've been to Africa on a mission trip and to parts of England, but that's as far as my international travel goes."

The mention of the black truck worried Frank, but there didn't seem to be any other red flags with Dr. Merritt. They thanked her and left, and then they headed back to his car. He glanced around as he unlocked the door, and the sight of a silver sedan parked across the street gave him pause. He couldn't positively identify it as the car he'd seen in Atlanta, but he couldn't rule it out, either. As he watched, a man in the front seat glanced in their direction. Frank turned and started walking toward the car, but before he'd gone ten feet, the car sped off and disappeared around the corner.

"Trouble?" Bailey asked, coming to his side.

"Looks like it. We're being followed again, and I'm sure Dr. Merritt is, as well." He pulled out his cell phone and reported to his team as they headed back to the car.

Once inside, his phone beeped with a text alert and he pulled up some photos and showed them to Bailey.

"We've uncovered two more known associates of the Balkavian murderers who killed your father. This is Jon Baltz and his partner Marc Weiner. They're both dangerous and armed. Keep an eye out."

"Sure thing." Bailey put on her seat belt as they pulled out of the parking lot. "Don't you think it's time you gave me my gun back? It could come in handy."

Kennedy shook his head. "No. I'm armed. If we have a problem, I'll protect you."

"I'm actually a good shot, Kennedy. I'm pretty good at protecting myself."

He didn't answer her and she let the subject drop. She knew it was doubtful that he would let her carry a gun while they were together—especially since he still didn't trust her. And why should he? The more she thought about her situation, the more the worry consumed her.

She didn't want to go back to prison. That much was certain. She wished she could go back in time to when her father was still alive and she didn't have a new punishment hanging over her head. A week. It had only been a week ago that her father was breathing and her life was on track. How could she have gotten so lost so quickly? And why was she so tempted to do the wrong thing the minute times got tough? She said a short silent prayer, asking God to help her in her weakness.

"What are you thinking?"

Kennedy's voice broke through her thoughts. She

needed to keep her mind on the here and now. She could muddle through these temptations later. She glanced at the side mirror as they drove up the ramp to the interstate and sat up abruptly. "I'm thinking there's a silver sedan following us again."

Kennedy noticed as well and pushed the accelerator. "Can you see the driver?"

"Yeah. He doesn't really look like either of those photos you showed me. Even so, I think we've rattled some cages with our investigation."

"It sure looks that way." Kennedy swerved into another lane, but the silver car didn't waver and was soon behind them again, closing in even as their speed increased. This time, the car didn't hang back but stayed right behind them. Bailey gripped the door as their pursuer hit their bumper. Her lips moved in silent prayer.

"Hold on," Kennedy said as he fought to control the car. The silver car bumped them again and then pulled up along Bailey's side of the car and rammed it.

She heard herself scream as metal screeched against metal. She could see the driver quite clearly, including the murderous glint in his eyes. This wouldn't end well.

Kennedy swerved to get away from him, and then he slowed and let the silver car go ahead of them. The reprieve didn't last long, however. The silver car braked too and veered, almost causing their car to run off the road to avoid crashing into it. Pebbles and dirt plumed under the tires as Kennedy fought for purchase on the asphalt. The next thing she knew, their pursuer was next to her again, this time hitting the right front fender. Their car bent under the impact and she could hear the tire shredding against metal. Their car spun around and, seconds later, the silver car crashed into the back door on Kennedy's side, pushing their car off of the road. It did one flip and then landed upright as smoke and dirt swarmed them. The silence that followed was deafening.

For a moment, she could do nothing as the pain sliced through her. The air bag had opened but done little to protect her from slamming against the car door during the wreck. She moaned and moved a bit, testing her arms and legs and finding that they still all worked and nothing was broken. She turned to the left.

"Kennedy! Kennedy, are you alright?" He moaned and a trail of blood ran down his face from multiple spots where the glass had scratched him. They weren't serious cuts, but he seemed to be struggling to stay conscious. She undid her seat belt and then reached for Kennedy's and undid it, but he barely moved when released. She squeezed his arm. "Kennedy?"

Suddenly, she saw a movement outside her window and she looked up. Fear swept over her like a wave. The driver from the other car was slowly getting out of his own wrecked vehicle and heading in their direction. He was about thirty feet away and, in his hand, he held a 9 mm pistol. He was slowly screwing a silencer on the barrel as he walked.

Oh God, please help us! Her plea was issued at the same time that she frantically shook Kennedy's body. "Kennedy? He's got a gun and he's coming this way!"

Kennedy moved and moaned under her prodding, but his eyes never opened. Panic flooded her and she turned and pushed against her car door, trying to escape. The metal scraped but opened far enough for her to wrench herself out. She fell to the ground but somehow managed to pull herself to her feet. She didn't want to leave Kennedy behind, but she couldn't move him, and he was unable to help himself. Hopefully, she could distract the shooter until Kennedy could revive himself and get away. She stumbled but headed toward the woods that lined the freeway, knowing that it was futile attempting to outrun a bullet, but she at least had to try.

FIFTEEN

The branches from the undergrowth tore at her pants, and at least four blackberry vines thrust their stickers into her legs, slowing her down, but she continued to run, darting around trees and bushes in her path. A bullet ripped into a tree by her left hand and she instantly pulled away as the splinters sprayed around her.

She zigzagged through another copse of trees, her breath searing her lungs. At the same time, an emptiness consumed her. Franklin Kennedy was probably dead. Either the crash would prove fatal and he would die from his injuries, or this mad man with the gun had already fired a bullet into his brain. Either way, his death left a hole in her heart that she hadn't expected. She wanted to curl into a ball and just accept the pain and emptiness she was feeling, but the man with the gun was too close for her to wallow in her grief. She stopped for a moment to rest, leaning against a large pine tree that she hoped shielded her body from view.

"Miss Cox, there's no place for you to go. Come back with me now. I won't hurt you."

Bailey struggled to catch her breath and grimaced at his words. Of course he was lying. He'd shoot her dead the second he could. She heard his footsteps on the forest floor. He was no more than thirty feet from her. A sense of desperation washed over her. He was right. There wasn't anywhere for her to go, and she was getting tired. Would her legs even carry her much farther?

"Miss Cox? Let's end this foolishness. You can't escape. Come out with your hands up and I promise no harm will come to you."

He was getting closer. This time when he spoke, she recognized that her pursuer had an accent, much like the men who had killed her father. Was this another Balkavian mercenary? It all made sense. Somewhere along the line, their inquiries must have hit the right chord. They had discovered a circle of crime much bigger than they'd expected, and the perpetrators were taking steps to end the investigation before their entire operation was put into jeopardy.

She gritted her teeth and pushed away from the tree, running in the opposite direction from the voice with the gun. She turned and headed back toward the road, effectively making a large circle, realizing that returning to the freeway might actually be her only chance at survival. Maybe she could flag down a passing motorist and escape.

A shot slammed into the wood by her shoulder and she ducked instinctively, barely missing the dangerous onslaught. The close call made her tap the last of her resources and put all the strength she could muster into her legs as she ran.

She snuck a look behind her and was instantly sorry she had done so. Her pursuer was even closer than she had realized. And while she was panicked and unsure, he was stepping deliberately as if he had all the time in the world. He smiled at her, making it blatantly obvious that he was enjoying the hunt and the knowledge that she had no chance of escape.

Some faint traffic noise caught her attention and she gave a quick prayer of thanks as hope surged within her. There hadn't been many cars on the road before, but surely someone would stop and give her a ride if she flagged them down.

The next bullet ripped into her skin on the side of her leg, about four inches above her right knee. She bit back the scream as the pain enveloped her, but she kept moving, dragging her wounded leg behind her. She had never felt such a horrible throbbing. It didn't look like it hurt this badly when folks got shot on TV...

The second bullet caught the same leg but lower. The pain was debilitating. She landed hard on her stomach, winded and with little strength to even crawl away from her pursuer. She felt like a rabbit caught in a snare—and could hear the hunter approaching. She knew he'd aimed his shots deliberately—injuries that would prevent her from running but still keep her alive. He didn't mean to kill her yet. She shuddered at the realization that he planned to take his time and truly savor the kill.

His steps were measured and slow. He knew she couldn't escape. She gritted her teeth, rolled over on her back and then pulled herself up to a sitting position the best she could and leaned against a nearby tree trunk. She knew she was going to die, but she didn't want the last thing she saw on this earth to be the dirt on the ground and the ants crawling along the leaves.

Her hunter was arrogant, and she could almost feel his conceit as he approached her slowly, drawing out the fear and feeding on the terror in her face. She watched him approach, her heart beating so hard she was sure he could hear that, as well. Its rapid pace was probably also giving him pleasure.

He was of medium build and was wearing black pants and a blue T-shirt. His hair was dark too, giving him an ominous appearance, even though his skin was pale and his lips stood out in contrast. Even his eyes were dark and seemed dead except for the glimmer of amusement.

"Did you enjoy your little run through the trees?" he said, smirking.

"You said you wouldn't hurt me. You're a liar. What a surprise."

He shrugged. "At least you made the game more interesting. I'll give you that." Once again, she registered the accent. This time, she was sure that this man spoke with the same accent as the men who had killed her father.

"I'm sorry it's just a game to you," Bailey whispered against the pain. "Someday you'll lose someone close to you, and then you'll understand how important life really is."

"That's where you're wrong. I don't let people close to me. I have no need for others." He raised his pistol and aimed it at her chest. "Good-bye, Miss Cox."

The gunshot sounded through the woods and she flinched, her mind taking a second to realize that the gunman hadn't fired with his silencer and that the shot she'd heard had come from *behind* her.

The dark man gazed down at his chest with a look of surprise, watching the blood form a circle on his shirt before he fell forward, landing on the ground a few feet away from Bailey. The light had already left his eyes by the time his body hit the dirt.

"Bailey? Bailey, are you okay?" She heard Kennedy first and then saw him approaching, his weapon still in his hands, smoke curling out of the barrel.

"Bailey!" Frank approached her at a run, pushing through pine straw and underbrush and ignoring the scratches. Bailey was still alive. That fact alone was reason to celebrate. But her blood was soaking the ground and her face was already growing pale.

"I thought you were dead," she said softly as he tore off his shirt and then ripped it into strips. She cried out as he moved her leg gently to tie the fabric around her wounds and staunch the bleeding.

"Shh. I'm okay. I've called for an ambulance and backup. They're both heading our way and should be here soon." He wiped away some of the blood from his own forehead and looked her in the eye. He could see the relief there radiating through the pain but was still surprised at the depth of feeling she expressed when she spoke.

"I'm so thankful to God that he didn't get you. I ran off because I wanted to distract him, but I was afraid he went to the car first and killed you anyway instead of following me."

Frank nodded. "I appreciate your efforts. I think he figured I was out of commission so he went after you first. He probably planned to circle back and finish me off before he escaped. His car is still operational. Ours is definitely totaled."

"Yeah," she said, laughing, but it turned into a grimace as she moved in a way that must have sent a sharp pain to her injuries. "That tends to happen when you roll it along the highway." She grabbed her leg above her wound and squeezed, and he stilled her hand by covering it with his own.

"Hang in there, Bailey. I'm going to get you out of here in one piece." He was glad she could find something to joke about after the latest attempt on their lives. If he'd arrived on the scene even a few seconds later… the result would have been heart-wrenching. Even now, he was having a hard time fighting the terror that had enveloped him when he'd discovered that Bailey had a killer chasing her through the woods. She had been smart to double back. That move alone had probably saved her.

He stood and checked the pulse of the shooter, verified that he was dead and then returned to Bailey's side. "Any clues that I missed while I was out?" he asked as he inspected her for other injuries. The two bullet wounds seemed the worst of it, and both were flesh wounds. Although he was sure they hurt, at least her leg wasn't broken—or worse. Still, she'd need stitches, crutches and rest before she'd be back on her feet again.

"He's one of our Balkavian friends," she said through her teeth. "He had the same accent as the men who killed my father."

"Anything else?"

She shook her head. "Not really. He wasn't the conversational type. Maybe his weapon will give us some clues, but I doubt it has a recognizable serial number left intact."

Frank leaned in close. He was overcome with relief and apprehension at the same time. What would life be like without Bailey Cox? The fact that he was even thinking along those lines scared him to death, but coming so close to losing her had driven home a point that he had been hesitant to even admit or analyze. He had feelings for Bailey Cox, and they were getting stronger every minute they spent together. He tried to push those thoughts aside and focus on the immediate situation. "Can you stand? I can probably get you to help faster if I can get you out of the woods."

"I can try, but I'm a mess. I'll get blood all over your clothes."

He glanced at his T-shirt and khakis, already spattered with his own blood and some broken glass. "These old things? No problem. You'll give me an excuse to go shopping." He put his arm behind her and slowly raised her to her feet. Once she was high enough, he swung her up in his arms and started carrying her toward the freeway, careful not to jostle her injured leg. She leaned against his shoulder and he found himself enjoying the contact. She was soft in all the right places and fit perfectly in his arms. She smelled good too—like the out-doors and a mixture of pine and tea olives.

Bailey laughed and broke his train of thought but didn't move her head. "Wait, did I just hear correctly? You *like* to go shopping?"

"I like to look professional. I get better results on cases when I do. Shopping isn't my all-time favorite activity, but it's necessary to reach my goal."

"I always thought you dressed well. You look too good to be a cop."

Frank stepped over a broken tree limb, again being extra careful of her injured leg.

"Thank you, I think. What's a cop supposed to look like?"

"Cheap, ill-fitting suits with wrinkles. Ugly ties. You know the stereotypes."

Frank laughed. "Wow. Maybe you should quit watching so much TV."

"Could be," she agreed, also with a smile. He was hoping their playful banter would take her mind off the pain in her leg and it seemed to be working for the most part. She still winced here and there as he carried her, but he wanted to get her away from the dead body in the woods and also close to the freeway so she could get help as soon as the ambulance arrived.

It wasn't long in coming. Only a few minutes after he'd set her down near the road, an ambulance pulled up and the EMTs rushed to her aid. He stepped back and let them do their work, watching carefully as they examined her wounds and loaded her into their vehicle. He jumped in the back as well and accepted some antiseptic wipes from one of the techs, which he used to wipe the blood away. Then the EMT spent a couple minutes putting some antibiotic medicine and butterfly bandages on his cuts. They weren't very deep but would probably have kept bleeding without treatment.

Once he was finished, Frank turned to Bailey and squeezed her hand. "I've got to stay here and finish the work at the scene just like before, but as soon as I'm done, I'll head over to the hospital. You'll probably need some stitches and who knows what else, but don't go anywhere until I get there. I'll pick you up, okay?"

She nodded and squeezed his hand back. "Want to give me my gun back now in case some unfriendly folks show up at the hospital?"

He laughed at her persistence, but her request wasn't really out of left field, considering what they'd both just been through. "I've already arranged for a uniformed officer to meet the ambulance and guard you at the hospital. You'll be safe there. I promise."

"What do you think all of this means?" she asked, motioning with her hands to both of their injuries and the wrecked car visible through the open ambulance doors.

He drew his lips into a thin line. "I think it means we're asking the right questions and we're making someone very nervous. Somebody wants us to quit this investigation, but that is *not* going to happen."

SIXTEEN

Bailey watched the blip on the heart monitor as it made its methodical way across the small blue screen. She was bored silly. She'd already been at the hospital for three hours. The doctors hadn't found any bullet fragments in her wounds, and there were no broken bones or damaged blood vessels, so they'd been able to stitch up her skin and dress the wounds without incident. They'd even covered her wounds with a waterproof dressing cover so she could shower. She wouldn't be running anywhere in the next few weeks, but it could have been so much worse that she was thankful a sore and swollen leg and a few battle scars were the only end results of her traumatic afternoon.

However, the relatively minor injuries meant she'd been patched up quickly, which left her plenty of time to sit and wait for Kennedy to come get her. Wait…and think…and worry.

Her newly diminished mobility couldn't have come at a worse time. The escalating attacks hinted that they were closing in on answers. But if the case would be closed soon, then she needed a plan for avoiding prison. The fake passport and IDs she'd ordered were ready and waiting for her to pick them up. They hadn't been cheap, and the balance owed would clean out her savings account completely. She hesitated and doubts assailed her. Kennedy was a really good detective and was way too good at reading her and her body language. Could she still afford to wait until after the case was completed before she ran? It would probably be safer to run now, before he realized what she was up to.

And what was she going to do about the Balkavians chasing her? The sooner she disappeared, the sooner they'd quit chasing her, right? Wouldn't they think that if she gave up the investigation, she was less of a threat? Or would they kill her anyway, just to tie up loose ends?

Should she leave now, run from the Balkavians *and* Kennedy and see how far she could get?

The mere thought sent a mix of adrenaline and dread spiking through her veins. Kennedy had vowed to hunt her down. Would he really do so over something as small as some stolen emails? Her mind replayed their earlier conversation, and a wave of certainty assailed her. Yes, he would. But that didn't mean he'd find her.

She thought about the officer guarding her door. He was young and inexperienced, so giving him the slip probably wouldn't prove to be too difficult, even in her injured condition.

She didn't know what to do and she wrapped her arms around her stomach, lost in thought. She'd made so many wrong decisions in her life that she desperately wanted to make the right one this time. She said a short prayer, asking for guidance and thanking God that she was still alive in the first place.

"How are we doing in here?" The nurse wore a smile and looked up from her clipboard as she entered the room.

"Just fine," Bailey replied, returning to the here and now and giving the nurse an innocent smile. "That pain medicine the doctor ordered really helped."

The nurse checked off something on the paperwork. "Good. Glad to hear it. Well, I'm here to check you out. Here's a prescription for more pain medicine." She went over the instructions as she handed the paper to Bailey along with the discharge information. She disappeared for a few minutes and then came back with a wheelchair and crutches. "You can take those crutches with you, but I have to wheel you down to the discharge area for pickup."

Bailey nodded. "Thanks." Thoughts swirled through her mind as the lady pushed her to the discharge area with her policeman guard following a few steps behind. They were almost to the waiting area when the officer stopped the nurse.

"Hold on. We can't take her into the general waiting area. I need a smaller room that is more secure. Do you have any options?"

The nurse nodded. "Sure." She wheeled Bailey into a side room that Bailey realized was the hospital chapel. The room was empty except for a few pews and a podium in the front. There was a cross on the wall and a small stained glass window that gave the room a cheerful ambiance. There was also a door at the rear of the room. The officer checked it to make sure it was locked and did a quick look around, but it was obvious the room was empty.

"Will this work?" the nurse asked.

"Sure thing. Thank you," the officer replied. They both helped Bailey get seated in a pew, and then the nurse left, taking the wheelchair with her.

Bailey motioned to the officer. "Have you heard from Detective Kennedy?"

The young man shook his head. He seemed like he'd just graduated high school and had an impish face with freckles that made him look even younger. "I'll give him a call and see how much longer he thinks it'll be."

The officer pulled out his cell phone and made the call while Bailey considered her surroundings. The main waiting room was just down the hallway, and, from what she remembered, it had an exit that led to the outside parking lot. There was always a row of taxis out by the front doors and she was tempted to find a way to lose the officer and just disappear into the city. Her stomach churned with indecision.

The officer turned and nodded in her direction. "Kennedy's about five minutes out."

She nodded and studied the room. She'd always thought stained glass was beautiful, and this window behind the podium was no exception. It portrayed an image of a dove that seemed to be surrounded by all the colors of the rainbow. She glanced at the cross and decided that some prayer was needed. It was no accident that she'd ended up here in the quaint chapel with some time on her hands. She bowed her head and was so in-

volved in her prayer that she didn't hear the door open.
After a few minutes, she looked up and saw Kennedy
sitting a couple of feet away. The other officer had left,
leaving the two of them alone. Kennedy had a strange
look on his face, one she couldn't quite decipher, and
his body language was tight and fatigued.

She was still here. He'd been sure she would have
evaded the officer and disappeared by now, but she was
in the chapel, still waiting for him. He couldn't believe it
and said his own prayer of thanks. She had been through
so much during this case that he really wouldn't have
blamed her if she'd tried to find somewhere safe to hide.

"How are you doing?" He hoped his eyes didn't con-
vey the worry he felt for her or the guilt that assailed
him. She had been hurt on his watch. He studied her
for a moment, reliving the fear he had gone through
when he'd seen her moments away from death. It had
terrified him, plain and simple. He moved closer until
he was sitting right beside her.

"I'm good. The doctors have me on some strong pain
meds. I won't be running a marathon for a while, but
I can't complain. Did you get everything wrapped up
at the scene?"

He rubbed his forehead absently. "Yes. You were
right. The dead man was Balkavian and a known associate of your father's killers. He had definite ties to
the Balkavian mercenary group we've been tracking."

"That was fast."

"Yeah, this one actually had an Interpol file, so we
were able to get quite a bit of good information about

him in record time. Those Interpol folks are being pretty helpful too, now that we've shown them several connections between our situation and some of the cases they've had over in Europe. Even the FBI is being helpful. The table is getting pretty full."

"We need to update our data map with all of this new information we've learned about the Balkavians, and I need a few uninterrupted hours on the internet to find some answers."

He nodded. "I agree, but right now I'm taking you someplace safe to rest. We'll hit the ground running first thing tomorrow."

She raised her eyebrow. "Someplace safe? Not home to your apartment?"

He ignored the slight thrill he felt at her referring to his apartment as home. "No. With this Balkavian threat, we'll have to go somewhere we're less likely to be expected or traced."

She touched his arm, evidently sensing his distress. "Are you okay?"

He looked into her eyes and was swept away into their sea-blue depths. "I wasn't completely honest with you, Bailey."

She frowned. "What do you mean?"

He paused and exhaled but finally spoke. "When we were talking about our families, I didn't tell you much about my mom and dad. I left out some pretty pertinent information."

"So tell me now."

He paused again, struggling. Finally, he pressed forward. "My dad, well, we're close. He practically raised me and my sister by himself. He had to, really. You see, my mom abandoned us when I was ten. One day she was there. The next day, she wasn't. She said she was going shopping, and she never came home."

Bailey took his hand and squeezed it. "I'm so sorry. What happened to her? Where did she go?"

"I didn't know at the time. My dad just turned into this unhappy shell of a man, and it took him years to recover. He's better now, but he's still not the same. Oh, he met our needs and we never went hungry when I was growing up, but his joy was gone. Once I became an adult and joined law enforcement, I searched for her until I found her. She's remarried and living out in California. She has a new family and doesn't care to acknowledge the one she left behind."

"Ouch."

"Yeah. Look, I know you've had it rough through the years—a lot worse than me. But I wanted you to know that about my family so you'd understand why I'm so…controlling. I thought I'd lost you today. That man came so close to taking your life, and then the entire time I was working the scene, I was convinced you'd run and wouldn't be here waiting for me at the hospital." Caught up in the moment—in the relief he felt that she was here, safe and hadn't left him—he gave her an exuberant kiss. Then, aware of the surprise on her face, he pulled back.

"I'm sorry. I'm just so relieved to see you. I was really worried." He brushed some stray hair away from her face. "Thank you," he said softly.

"For what?" Her voice was soft, as well.

"For waiting for me. For being here."

She was so quiet that he pulled back to look at her. He could see the distress on her face, and a sickening feeling swept over him. "What's wrong?"

"Nothing."

"It doesn't seem like nothing. Come on. You're my partner on this, right? Partners talk. I need to know what you're thinking." He leaned back against the seat, dread tightening the muscles in his chest.

She raised an eyebrow. "Am I? Your partner?"

"Yes." He didn't hesitate.

She did.

He nudged her on. "Look, I failed mind reading in college. In fact, I've never been any good at it."

He got the desired result. She gave a small smile but didn't look up at him. "As long as we're being honest, I should tell you I *was* thinking of running. Your instincts are pretty good."

He sat back, disappointed that she had been plotting and even more surprised that she had shared that fact. She had to know that her honesty would change things between them. Yet, once again, she had opted for honesty over subterfuge. That was a good thing, even if hearing the truth hurt. Every muscle in his body seemed to tighten. "Why?"

She sat back as well and moved a few inches away from him. "Why? Because I'm scared."

"Scared of the Balkavians?"

"Scared of going back to prison," she blurted out. "There, I've said it." She looked away from him again. "Look, I understand. There are consequences for my actions. I broke the law. I have to pay the price. But prison is a dangerous place, and sometimes you have to do pretty dangerous things just to survive."

Frank was silent for a moment, considering her words. Although his boss had promised leniency, the odds were that she would spend at least some time behind bars. After all, her act had been a felony, and this wasn't her first offense. "I can't promise you won't have to do time, Bailey."

"I know that. I didn't expect you to. I did this to myself and it's my own fault. You're a straight arrow, Kennedy. I admire that about you, even when it's me you're forcing to toe the line. But knowing all of that doesn't erase my fear."

His hands clenched. "You promised you'd stay. You gave me your word." He forced his voice to be soft and nonthreatening, despite the tension he was feeling inside.

"That's why I haven't run yet. That's why I'm here, praying for direction so I don't make another giant mistake." She rubbed her eyes and left her hand covering them, almost as a shield. "I don't know what to do. I'm so mixed up inside. And I'm sorry. I'm so sorry that I've disappointed you."

She reached for her crutches and started to stand, and he took her hand and helped her to her feet. He could feel her muscles tense and could tell she was fighting her own personal battle. He also knew instinctively that this was one decision that she had to make on her own. He wanted her to make the right choice because *she* wanted to, not because he was standing behind her with the cuffs in his hand.

He pulled back and gently rubbed her cheek. "Please stay, Bailey. I can't promise you it will be an easy road ahead, but I can promise you won't go down it alone." He met her eyes and held them. "Please stay."

He didn't expect an answer and didn't force her to give one. He could see the battle still going on in her eyes. As hard as it was for him to do, he had to take a step back.

And if she made the wrong decision, he was determined to follow through on his promise to hunt her down. He bent down to tie his laces, and at the same time reached over and put a small black dot on her shoe. It looked like a smudge of dirt, barely noticeable, but it was actually a very powerful GPS device. He'd been carrying it around with him for a few days, hoping he wouldn't have to use it, but now, he was done taking chances.

SEVENTEEN

Bailey touched her lips absently as she read the notice that had just popped up on her screen, once again letting her know that her fake passport and IDs were ready for pickup. It was her third notice. It was encrypted and looked like it came from a message board about pet care, but to her, it was easy to recognize.

She posted a reply, delaying the meeting time. With her current injuries and hampered mobility, she wasn't sure when or how she'd get her documents, but somehow she would manage. She quickly deleted the notice and slowly turned her head around to see if Kennedy had noticed. She was relieved to see that he was still busy with a call on his cell phone.

Kennedy had rented them adjoining hotel rooms at an out-of-the-way hotel designed for long-term stays. Her suite contained a couch, table and chairs, and a small kitchenette along with a bedroom. Apparently, they used this hotel as a safe house for witnesses and the like. It was simple but served the purpose well, and it was a lot nicer than many of the places she had lived in when she'd been growing up. It was definitely cleaner.

She wondered fleetingly if it was going to bother him to have her out of his sight when they were sleeping in separate rooms, especially after their conversation at the hospital, but so far he had said nothing more about it. She shook her head as she glanced in his direction. He'd probably be standing at the door all night, wondering if she would still be there in the morning, but, to his credit, he had at least allowed her to have her privacy.

She was still surprised that Kennedy had shared so much with her yesterday about his family. His mother's abandonment explained a lot about his behavior and need for control, and she could tell that it was a subject that he shared with very few. It also made her realize how much it would hurt him if she ran and tried to disappear. That was a side of her decision that she hadn't really considered until now.

The kiss had been even more surprising. She touched her lips again, remembering. It had been precious and sweet and quite enjoyable after she got over the shock of realizing that her own feelings for Franklin Kennedy were stronger than she had ever imagined. That fact made her decision about running even harder to make.

She couldn't put a finger on the exact moment when her attraction had begun, but she had to acknowledge that her feelings were very much engaged. He had promised to support her regardless of the future and be by her side. That was something no one had ever done for her before. How could she leave that behind? She didn't know what the future held for her and Kennedy, but it was very tempting to stay and find out. And no matter what happened, she was thankful that he'd kissed her. Very thankful. The entire day yesterday had made her see Franklin Kennedy with new eyes.

"Ready for the update?"

She nodded at him and set her computer aside. "Sure thing."

"Interpol has confirmed that Dr. Petrela never attended medical school in Balkavia. The diploma hanging on his wall is fake, along with the rest of his credentials. Apparently, he was a paramedic in Balkavia, so he did have some medical training, and he was also a member of the BLU. We took a look at his financials and discovered he's been living way above his reported means. We haven't been able to discover too much more about him, but we just sent a team to go bring him in for questioning, and he's cleared out."

Bailey swallowed. "*Cleared out?* What exactly does that mean?"

"It means he and his family are nowhere to be found, and his bank account has been emptied, as well. My guess is they're on the run and have returned to Europe." He winked at her. "He probably ended up in one of those Communist dictatorships that don't participate in extradition."

She made a face at his reference and he laughed and continued. "In any case, since he's disappeared, the threat against us might have lessened. In fact, their failure to silence us might be why he cut his losses and disappeared."

He handed her his iPad, which had a man's picture on it. She shivered at the sight of a face she would never forget. Just seeing the man's eyes again sent chills down Bailey's back.

"Meet Hashim Berisha. He's the gentleman who tried to kill us yesterday." She handed him back the iPad. "As I told you before, he's got definite links to the Balkavian Liberation Union. Apparently, he was under suspicion for being one of the officers involved in the Farmhouse Scandal that occurred during the war."

"Farmhouse Scandal?" Bailey asked. The phrase rang a bell, but she couldn't remember the details.

Kennedy swiped the front of his iPad and handed it back to her. It showed a grainy picture of a small farmhouse, surrounded by muddy, dark fields. A few unnamed men stood around the building, most of them holding cigarettes. The faces were hard to see, but the guns in their hands stood out.

"The Farmhouse Scandal refers to the organ-harvesting ring that was operating a makeshift clinic in this farmhouse near Vakamira, Balkavia, a few years ago during their civil war. Apparently, the BLU would take both civilians and enemy soldiers to this clinic, harvest the needed organs and then kill them. Once the victims' organs were harvested, they were transported to Turkey and sold. If I had to guess, I'd say Dr. Petrela was somehow involved."

Bailey shuddered. "That's so horrible. Were these men never brought to justice?"

Kennedy shook his head. "The United Nations started an investigation, but it never went anywhere. When it was clear they were losing the war, the bloodier elements of the BLU went underground. Many of the really dangerous men were never found, and many had been using false names. Several people, including Berisha, and some doctors were labeled in absentia as war criminals and are wanted for questioning by the UN. It looks like after the war, Berisha joined a group of Balkavian mercenaries and has been committing crimes in both Europe and the US for the past fifteen years."

"I don't see either Berisha or Petrela in this photo."

"It's not a great photo and it's hard to identify the men, but, even so, I'm sure there were a lot more soldiers involved than those pictured there. Interpol is working on the identification."

"So Berisha was working with Dr. Petrela?" She put the iPad down on the table this time. The information Kennedy was telling her was sickening and caused a pain in her stomach. How could someone charged with helping others choose to do so much harm? It was inconceivable. She thought back to the interview she'd had with Dr. Petrela and couldn't imagine the man she'd met as the leader of an organ-harvesting ring or a criminal organization. Still, people only showed others what they wanted them to see. She'd certainly learned that lesson over the course of her life.

"It looks that way, but we're still short on proof. Dr. Petrela's background is sketchy at best, but it's a pretty big coincidence that he was over there when this was going on if he wasn't involved. Like I said, Interpol is still trying to get photographic evidence of the farmhouse medical staff since the UN dropped the investigation. What we think we're dealing with here is a group of these BLU leaders who banded together after the war to provide mercenary services. So far, Berisha and these two, Adrian Bekim and Edon Vekaric—" he pulled out a paper file and pointed to the pictures of the two men who had caused her father's death "—have all been linked to the BLU and to each other."

He closed the file and set it aside, presumably to spare her further pain. "What we are thinking is that our Balkavian group is still involved in illegal organ trafficking in Europe. Interpol is handling that part of the investigation. But we think the same group is laundering their money here in the US. They've set up an operation right along the Eastern Seaboard and are still using ex-BLU soldiers for guards and assassins to protect their interests."

He paused and took a few steps to the right, where he pointed to Bailey's father's picture. "We also think your father here in Jacksonville stumbled across this scheme, at least part of it, when he was investigating the candidates for the CEO position at Gates Industries, and was killed to make sure his findings were never discovered. We also think that these mercenaries believe that you—" he motioned in her direction with his hands "—and I are a threat to their criminal activity, and this explains all of the attacks against us."

Bailey's mind was spinning. Everything Kennedy was saying was making sense. What they needed now was proof. "Is Gates already involved with the money laundering, or was Petrela trying to use it for that purpose?" she asked.

"That's a good question. We sent over a forensic accounting team there a few hours ago, with a warrant from Judge Sanders. We should know soon enough."

He shifted. "Either way, if Dr. Petrela is our perp, it's likely that he's the one who ordered your father's death and is responsible for the death of Gabriel Jeffries."

"Do you think Jeffries was killed because he was the top contender for the job at Gates?"

Kennedy nodded. "It sure looks that way. We'll know a lot more if and when we catch up with Petrela and get the results of our subpoena from Gates."

"Are the other candidates still in danger?"

"The last name on the list, Dr. Marty Entemann, has withdrawn his application and gone into hiding, with law enforcement's knowledge and blessing. Clarissa Merritt has also taken a leave of absence from her current position for her safety. We tried to get Dr. Fredericks to do so as well, but he's convinced he can handle it himself. He's hired two personal bodyguards."

"I think I might be able to find out even more about this now that we have a better idea of what we're looking for." She pulled her laptop into her lap.

Kennedy leaned back and said nothing more as Bailey's fingers started flying over the keyboard. *Vakamira, Balkavia. BLU. Farmhouse case.* She found a site connected to an American journalist's book on the scandal. He had interviewed several of the BLU soldiers who had transported both victims and body organs. There were also vague references to a surgeon who performed the medical procedures, but he wasn't named, or even described with any clarity. Could that have been the mysterious Dr. Petrela?

She scanned more documents, but still no name or pictures of the doctor surfaced. All she found was that the physician was described as a Balkavian from the village of Revnik. She kept reading. Another site said since there was minimal evidence, no bodies found and few witnesses, then the allegations must be false. Still another site claimed that the bodies did exist, but they had been buried under false names and the local villagers had refused to allow any exhumation or collection of evidence.

"Wow, there's a lot of conflicting information out there, but there's one thing that keeps getting mentioned—this doctor from Revnik who was in charge of the illegal operations. I wonder if Dr. Petrela is the mysterious doctor or if he was just one of the lower-level paramedics who helped out…" She gave Kennedy a summary of what she was finding and he listened intently.

"If Petrela is this doctor who you're describing, that would sure explain a lot," Kennedy agreed. "The need to keep his identity hidden from the world was certainly reason to kill, especially if he was trying to take over a large, multinational corporation so he could launder the funds from his illegal operations in Europe."

The words swirled in Bailey's mind as her fingers continued to fly across the keyboard. They had a lot of conjecture but still no proof. She searched for the next several minutes but could find no other hints to the man's identity.

"Look," she said, her voice filling with excitement. "We know what Petrela looks like, and surely he's using a fake name. If I can just find some photographic evidence from the Farmhouse case, I might be able to catch a glimpse of the mysterious doctor and see if the faces match. Then we'll have the proof we need. Even if he's fled, if we can build a case, law enforcement around the world will be aware of what he did and will be trying to bring him to justice. I can set up searches that will scour several different databases looking for the photos or the other identifying evidence that we need."

Kennedy's face became more animated, as well. "That's a great idea. How long do you think it will take to find something?"

Bailey shrugged. "It could be minutes. It could be days. I'm not finding much of anything with my usual searches here so it might take a while, but it's worth digging deeper." On several databases, she set the search for photos of soldiers and civilians who might have been involved in the BLU killings. Then she also set alerts. "Okay, you and I both will be notified if anything comes up."

Frank stood and came to sit beside her on the couch. He was close and touched her chin lightly with his finger and moved her head to face him. "You're amazing. Do you know that?"

She shook her head. "I'm not amazing. I'm a criminal."

"That's the past," he said softly.

"The past, yes, and my future. Even if I never commit another crime, I'm still going back to jail."

He ran his fingers gently down the side of her face, wishing he could erase the unhappiness he saw. "That doesn't have to set the course for the rest of your life.

You've changed, Bailey. Look at all of the good work you've done on this case. You've been a real asset, but there's more. I see your heart. I see how hard you are trying to make good decisions. You're not the same girl I knew six years ago."

She bit her lip but didn't say anything, so he continued. "I'm not going to desert you, Bailey. Yes, you have to face the consequences of what you did, but I'll be right there beside you." He leaned back and pulled something from his pocket. It was a small, wrapped package with a tiny gold string.

She raised an eyebrow. "What's this?"

"Just a small gift. Nothing fancy, but it made me think of you."

Her hand was trembling a bit as she turned it over and over. She didn't rush to open it and a part of him wondered why. It was almost like she was cherishing the act itself, rather than the present inside the package. He thought through her history. She probably hadn't been on the receiving end of too many gifts during her life, and he suddenly vowed that he was going to change that. He would treat her like the precious gift she was to him, if she'd let him.

"What is it?"

He shrugged nonchalantly. "Open it and find out."

She carefully untied the ribbon and pulled aside the tissue paper to reveal a small, golden pin. She looked up, her eyes moist. "It's a bird. It's really pretty."

"Ah, but it's not just any bird." He took it from her and gently pinned it on her shirt near her collar. "This is a very special bird—a phoenix. Have you ever heard of them?"

She shook her head and looked down at the pin. "No. What's so special about them?"

"A phoenix is a bird from Greek mythology. It's a beautiful creature with brilliant colors, just like you. When it dies, it burns up in magnificent flames and then is reborn and rises up from the ashes, leaving the past behind. It's a symbol of starting fresh. That's just what you're doing now as you enter this new chapter of your life—leaving the ashes behind and starting over."

She fingered the pin and then looked at him with appreciation in her eyes. "That was really nice of you."

He leaned forward and kissed her gently on the forehead, and then he pulled back and stood. "I hope you have a good evening and get lots of rest. I'll be next door if you need me."

She nodded. "Thank you for the pin."

He paused by the door and gave her a smile. "You're very welcome."

EIGHTEEN

Bailey sat near the back of the conference room at the sheriff's office, her injured leg propped up on a chair in front of her, her computer on her lap and her crutches on the floor. She ran her fingers slowly over her new phoenix pin, once again remembering the tenderness that Kennedy had displayed the evening before. He seemed to really care about her, and the thought made her feel warm from head to toe.

What did she feel for him? She was definitely attracted to him. The realization made her laugh, considering everything that had happened between them over the last six years or so. If someone would have told her that she'd have romantic feelings for him back when he had first cuffed her and hauled her off to jail, she would have denied it to her dying breath.

Could they have a future together? Did she love him? She had experienced so little love in her life that she wasn't sure how to label the feelings that bombarded her whenever he was close. She did know that her heart sped up when he was near, and she could feel herself blush when he gave her a compliment. She also remembered how empty she had felt when she'd thought he had been shot by the roadside.

She glanced to the front of the room where Kennedy and a team of other law enforcement officers were about to begin a briefing on the case. Their eyes met and electricity seemed to sizzle between them.

A notice popped up on her laptop and grabbed her attention. It was a tersely written—though still coded—reminder that her fake ID documents were ready for pickup. This one had a stern note that demanded she meet with the provider immediately. She quickly erased the notice, her muscles tense. She glanced around nervously to see if anyone had noticed, but no one was paying any attention to her.

After short introductions, the team started giving everyone the basic facts of the case, starting with her father's death. She tried to tune in to the discussion around her and push her other thoughts aside, but it was hard to keep her mind on the case, especially when someone else was talking and Kennedy's eyes found hers. His look was intense but in a positive way, as if he wanted to share every moment with her. The look sent goose bumps down her arm. She smiled and shyly looked away, unwilling to encourage him further until she had made a decision about what her next move should be.

An FBI agent suddenly stood and drew her attention. He passed out a small packet to everyone in the room, including her, and then started speaking from the front of the room. She sorted through the contents, noting that several crime scenes were depicted with a short description under the photos.

"Interpol recently sent us information about the death of a Turkish doctor who was wanted for committing war crimes and illegal organ transplants in the 2000s. We believe he worked with the doctor in Balkavia during the war and was the doctor's primary contact for the organ sales. We also think that our BLU group believed he was a liability and chose to reduce their risk of exposure by murdering him. They are probably also responsible for the deaths of these two men—" he gestured toward some of the pictures "—who were killed in New York." He motioned to another photo. "And this man who was killed in Chicago. These victims were all involved in pharmaceuticals, mostly in distribution, and were all implicated in a money-laundering scheme."

He paused and flipped to a new page in his packet. "That operation has all but disintegrated since their deaths, which explains why the group might be looking at Gates to be a replacement. We're still investigating Gates to see if they had any involvement."

A text message suddenly popped up on her screen.

I have your package. Meet me outside by the large oak tree across the street. Now. Or else.

Her contact must be getting nervous. Regardless of what she decided to do, she still had to pay for the services she had requested. If not, there would be severe consequences. She hit a few keys and authorized the payment, then glanced around once again to see if anyone had seen her screen. Thankfully, everybody's attention was focused on the FBI agent again, and nobody seemed to notice when she set her computer aside, grabbed her purse and her crutches, and headed outside. She passed by several law enforcement officers and civilians as well, as she made her way out of the sheriff's office building, but nobody stopped her or talked to her, and for that she was grateful.

She paused at the doors and looked to both sides and behind her, but there still didn't seem to be anyone following or observing her. With a deep breath, she pushed through the doors, shielding her eyes for a moment as they adjusted to the sunshine. She crossed the street, constantly aware of everyone and everything around her. There was an old couple playing checkers at one of the picnic tables and a few moms and small children enjoying the slide and swing set in the play area. Nobody was paying any attention to her. She saw the oak and headed that way. As she approached, a middle-aged man came around the trunk and startled her.

"Hey, Bailey."

She smiled when she recognized him. "Hey yourself, Houston. Did you get what I needed?" There was no use telling her contact that she wasn't sure if she even wanted the new IDs anymore. She'd agreed to buy his product, and he'd delivered…so now she had to do her part. Even if she decided not to run, she still had to pick up the documents. Houston was well connected. If she left him in the lurch, it would haunt her for several years to come in more ways than she could imagine.

Houston had a small cherry cigar in his mouth and

he smiled and transferred the small butt to the other side as he talked. "Don't I always? You know you can count on me." He raised an eyebrow, apparently not in as much of a hurry as she'd thought. "What'd you do to your leg?"

"Tried to catch a bullet with it."

"I thought you were smarter than that."

She laughed, not wanting to say the wrong thing since he still had her packet. It was always in her best interests to agree with Houston and his opinions. She knew his temper could be...volatile, though he'd always treated her well. For the most part anyway. Houston was reliable, but he was also bad about changing his prices and trying to get some extra bucks out of her before each transaction was completed. Today was no exception.

"Look, Bailey. I had to put a rush on these. You didn't give me much turnaround time. That kind of rush costs more. Plus, you made me wait awhile before pickup. It was a huge inconvenience." He took a long draw on his cigar and sent out three puffs in rings of smoke that rose slowly into the sky.

She met his eye. "Then I hope you'll be able to sell them to somebody else with my picture on them. I already told you I couldn't go higher on this job. You've cleaned out my savings. I can't give you what I don't have."

She'd figure out what to do with them later, but for now she just wanted to finish this transaction and go back inside to her computer so she could work some more on finding the doctor from Revnik. The more she thought about it, the more she was convinced that he was the key to this entire case, if she could just find proof that it was Petrela.

Her thoughts turned to Kennedy—how pleased he'd be if she could find the proof she was seeking. And how disappointed he'd be if he knew what she was doing right now. Her thoughts swirled in her head as she waited for Houston to decide his next move.

Houston seemed to consider her words for a minute as he took yet another drag from his cigar. He finally threw the butt on the concrete and ground the coals out with his heel. "Alright, alright. We'll let it go this time." He pulled out a manila envelope and handed it to her. "I just received your payment through the usual channels. We're good. And don't forget to mention me to your friends."

She almost laughed at that one. She doubted he would still want her to do that if he knew she was working so closely with the sheriff's office. And now the FBI was involved. Wouldn't that throw him for a loop? She opened the envelope and examined the passport and driver's license. They were excellent quality, just as she'd expected. "Melissa Jackson? That's the best name you could come up with?"

He smiled, showing a row of yellow teeth. "Beggars can't be choosers. She died a few years back in a boating accident and is about your age, height and weight. I even threw in a couple of free credit cards to help you get your trip underway."

She put the envelope in her purse and nodded. Even though she could be headed to prison, she might as well leave him thinking that she was still planning a new life in an exotic land. There was no reason to shatter the illusion. "Thanks, Houston. You always were a class act. I'll actually miss you, you know?"

He punched her in her arm good-naturedly as his face flushed. "Stay safe, kid. Okay?"

"That's the plan."

He turned and left, pulling out a new cigar and lighting it up as he walked, and she watched him go, a tinge of unexpected sadness hitting her. She was telling the truth when she said she'd miss Houston. They'd done business several times as she was growing up, and he had always been kind to her, even if he was a tad on the greedy side.

She fingered the documents, looked them over one more time and then put them back in the envelope. She had to make a decision. It was time. She stood still for several minutes, letting the thoughts roll around in her mind, and then she pulled out a pen and small notepad from her purse. She wrote a short note and tucked it in with the IDs. Then she addressed the outside of the envelope, which she sealed shut. Finally, she stored it back in her purse. She turned to go back to the sheriff's department building when a lady walking a small dog approached her. The woman smiled and Bailey smiled in return, but her smile disappeared when she saw the pistol the woman was holding, equipped with a silencer on the end. The woman dropped the dog leash and motioned with her free hand.

"Hello, Ms. Cox. You need to come with me."

Bailey's pulse sped up and she grimaced. "Do I have a choice?" The woman was only a few feet away. Any shot she took was sure to be deadly. Bailey could tell that the woman had no qualms about shooting her and leaving her body right here in the park. Bailey could probably knock the gun out of her hands with one of her crutches, but the woman would no doubt win any contest of strength given Bailey's current physical condition, and others around them might get hurt in the process if she tried to escape.

Her eyes swung over to the group of children playing on the playground, all oblivious to the danger. At least if she went with the woman, there was some chance of escaping later on, and no one else would get hurt. She gripped the strap on her purse and bit her bottom lip, wishing once again that she had been able to talk Kennedy into letting her carry her gun again.

"No, you don't have a choice. And if you give me any trouble, my first bullet goes in you, and the next five will go into those kids over there." She motioned with the gun and Bailey followed her obediently through the park and away from the law enforcement building. Bailey took a moment to look behind her to see if anyone else had noticed her abduction, but nobody was paying any attention, and the woman moved closer and jabbed the pistol against her ribs. "This isn't a game, Cox. I'll shoot you right here if I have to, as well as the innocent bystanders. Now move."

Bailey nodded and continued forward again, leaning heavily on her crutches. "I hear that accent in your voice," she ventured. "You wouldn't happen to be from Balkavia, would you?"

"Shut up and move," the woman said roughly. This time, the woman hit her so hard in her back that she was sure she'd have a bruise tomorrow. If she lived that long.

NINETEEN

Frank glanced again at Bailey's computer, which was still sitting at the table in the back where she had been sitting. Where had she gone? He'd noticed her get up and leave the room, but he figured she was visiting the ladies' room. Now she had been gone too long, and he was starting to worry. She couldn't have planned to leave for the day or she would have taken her computer with her and hopefully also let him know where she was going. Even though the Balkavian's attack in the woods had ended well, she was still in danger and would be until this case was wrapped up for good. Surely she would realize that and not do anything foolhardy.

The briefing ended and he motioned to Sergeant Daniels, who was nearby holding a cup of coffee.

"Sergeant, can you help me out for a minute?"

"Sure, Detective. What can I do for you?"

Frank motioned toward Bailey's computer. "Bailey Cox was just here a moment ago. She stepped out and didn't return. Can you check her computer to see if there are any clues as to where she's gone?"

Daniels shrugged. "I can try. Do you have her password?" He set his mug down and lifted the lid on the computer, which instantly came to life.

"No, but I'm worried about her. I'm wondering if she got an email or other message that pulled her away from the briefing."

Daniels hit a few keys but shook his head. "Without the password, I can't break in, at least not right away. I have some software that will help us get access, but it takes a while. Do you have time to wait?"

"Not really, but go to it anyway. I'll keep looking while you try to break through. Call my cell if you get anywhere."

"Understood. Okay if I take this to my desk?"

"Sure thing."

Daniels stood and took the laptop and power converter with him, and Frank put his hands on his hips and turned, looking for any other clue that would help him discover what had happened to Bailey. She wouldn't run now when they were so close to solving this mess, right? With Interpol's and the FBI's help, they were finally getting some answers to their questions.

He checked his cell phone on the off chance that she had called or texted but didn't see any missed alerts. There was a new message in his email, however. He opened it and a sinking feeling swept over him. Each word in the message seemed to burn into his brain.

Right after Matt Cox had been killed, Frank had put an alert on Bailey's bank account that would tell him if she withdrew any large sums of money. Apparently, about half an hour ago, she had withdrawn the bulk of her savings, leaving only a few hundred dollars. He hadn't seen the alert before now because he had been involved in the briefing.

Anger and frustration surged through his veins. She had run. She had broken her word, cleaned out her account and disappeared. Pain sliced through him, reminding him of the feelings he'd had when he'd first realized his mother wasn't coming back. It was a raw, searing pain, so strong that it made him stagger. He pulled out a chair and sat, surprised at the depth of feeling her betrayal had caused.

For the first time since he had run into Bailey that night in the alley, he admitted to himself that he was falling in love with her. He had been fighting against those feelings ever since that night, yet he had lost the battle completely. He was in love with Bailey Cox, and she had just run out on him. Would he never learn his lesson?

Suddenly he stood. He had promised to find her if she ran, and he fully intended to follow through. He found Graham and told him what had happened, and Graham alerted the rest of the team while Frank found his iPad and pulled up the program that linked to the GPS transponder he had put on Bailey's shoe. He had been a fool, but at least the precautions he'd taken meant he didn't have to let Bailey get away with her betrayal.

The transponder was working. The program came up with a map of the local area and a small red dot blinked at him. According to the program, Bailey was traveling north over one of the Jacksonville bridges.

His phone rang and he answered the call, noticing that it was Ben Graham on the other end. "I'm at the front desk looking at the security cameras, and there's something you've got to see."

"I'll be right there." He hung up his phone, grabbed his iPad and then headed as fast as he could to the front desk. He found Ben in the room behind the desk, where the security officer had nine screens connected to cameras that rotated and filmed different areas of the building. Ben pointed to the center screen and spoke to the officer in charge. "Okay, run it again."

The officer complied and Frank watched as the camera panned across the park. He could see Bailey as clear as day meeting up with a man who was smoking a small cigar. His eyes widened as he watched her take the packet, examine the contents, write on the envelope and put it in her purse. He only caught a glimpse of the contents as she examined them. One of the items looked like a passport, and although it was hard to tell for sure, his heart still sank. Another wave of betrayal and disappointment swept over him and he shook his head and took a step back.

"Hang on, Frankie. This is where it gets interesting," Ben said, giving him a nudge. Frank didn't respond right away and Ben nudged him again. "Watch the lady with the dog. See her?"

Frank nodded and then took a step closer to the screen. "Is that a gun?"

Ben nodded. "Sure looks like one to me. Nine mil is my guess. Bailey's been abducted. And if I had to guess, I'd think her abductor probably speaks Balkavian."

"I'd think the same thing." He opened his iPad as his emotions swirled within him. Okay, she had bought falsified documents, but she hadn't left the area on her own accord, and now she was in danger. She'd probably been planning to leave before she was interrupted, but he'd worry about that later. Right now, his primary objective was saving her life.

"I'm tracking her with the GPS. We've got to get her back now before the Balkavians decide she's too much of a liability."

Ben looked surprised at the GPS information but didn't hesitate. "Understood." He immediately got on the phone and coordinated the team for a search and rescue as he and Frank headed toward the equipment room. They said little as they suited up in body armor. A few short minutes later, the team of five from the Jacksonville Sheriff's Department were headed after Bailey in two separate vehicles—Ben and Frank in Frank's new unmarked Dodge Charger and the other three in a large van filled with surveillance and other equipment.

Frank had tried to drive, but Ben had refused to let him in no uncertain terms. "You're too involved in this case," Ben had admonished, and now, as he rode after Bailey, praying that she was still alive, Frank was starting to accept that truth. He *was* too involved, and it was a good thing he wasn't driving.

He was actually glad that Ben hadn't considered Frank's attachment reason enough to leave him behind, because if the positions had been reversed, he would have at least considered doing that to Ben. Law enforcement and emotion didn't mix, and right now he needed to be at the top of his game if he wanted to save Bailey from the Balkavians. He wasn't foolish enough to imagine that they would ever have a life together. Bailey obviously didn't want him since she'd chosen to run. But if he could save her life, then at least he could offer her one more chance to get her life on track. It wasn't much, but he would have to settle for having her alive at the end of the day.

He got a new notification on his phone and pulled it up quickly as Ben maneuvered around the traffic. A picture slowly uploaded, showing a group of soldiers in front of a farmhouse. He looked at the message Bailey had attached to the search, and immediately understood that she was hoping to find a picture of the mysterious Balkavian doctor from Revnik. He scanned the photo but didn't recognize any of the faces. Hopefully, the search Bailey had started would keep going and find other photos. He stowed his phone as Ben took a particularly quick turn that slammed him into the car door a little harder than he'd expected.

He couldn't complain. Ben was driving like Bailey's life depended upon it.

And it did.

Bailey pulled against the plastic zip tie that bound her hands, but there was no escaping it. She had nothing to cut it with and didn't see anything sharp that she could rub it against. They had thrown her unceremoniously into the back of a van, and her captor was seated a few feet away, her gun still pointed in Bailey's direction. Every now and then, her abductor turned and said something to the driver, but it was all in Balkavian, and Bailey had absolutely no idea what they were saying to each other. She had a deep sense of foreboding since they hadn't bothered to cover their faces. Obviously, their plan was to kill her because they weren't worried that she could identify them.

She felt the van slow and then make a series of turns. There wasn't much light anyway, but it suddenly got much darker as if they had gone underground. She imagined that they were in some sort of parking garage. Finally, the van stopped completely, the woman got out, and then turned and motioned with her gun.

"Out. Now."

"Where are we going?"

"Just shut up and do what I tell you." The woman's tone left no room for argument, and since Bailey wasn't getting anywhere with her questions, she decided to comply. She'd met plenty of women like this in prison—tough as nails, both on the inside and outside. Her threats to hurt Bailey for failing to cooperate were not bluffs—she meant every word. When Bailey had been incarcerated and had time to work on the relationship, women like this would eventually crack and come to a mutual understanding with her: they'd leave each other alone as long as they stayed out of each other's way. But Bailey doubted there was time to get that far with this woman. If her guess was correct, she would be dead by nightfall.

She maneuvered herself out of the van and lifted her hands so the woman could cut the bindings, but the woman shook her head.

"Look, I can't walk without them. I need to use my crutches," she said, putting all her weight on her good leg. "Do you want to carry me to wherever we're going?" Finally, the woman relented, pulled a knife that Bailey hadn't even seen from her waistband and cut the plastic ties. Bailey leaned over and grabbed her crutches, and then she followed the driver toward a door near the outside wall that led to an elevator. The woman followed her with the gun trained on her midriff the entire time, and Bailey knew the chances of escaping this situation were getting slimmer by the minute.

Even if she were able to disable the woman, and that was a big *if,* the driver was still heavily armed. She could see both his pistol strapped to his waist and a knife in a scabbard by his thigh. And those were only the weapons that were visible. There was no telling what else he had hidden on his body. He undoubtedly was another of the mercenaries in the group, which likely meant he was also a trained fighter. She had done some basic survival street fighting in her day but was sure she couldn't hold a candle to this man's experience and skill.

The three of them entered the elevator in silence, went up several floors and then stepped out once the elevator opened up to a well-manicured office reception area. The secretary said nothing to any of them, but it was clear they were expected. She hit a buzzer under her desk, and Bailey heard a click as a heavy wooden door on her right unlocked. The driver pushed through and held the door as she passed, and she heard a click as the door relocked behind her.

The woman led them down a short hallway, her pistol perpetually ready to ward off any attack Bailey could attempt. They went into a large office and the door swung shut and locked behind them. A man was standing behind a desk talking on his phone with his back to them, but when he heard them enter, he quickly finished his call and turned, giving Bailey a smile.

"Good afternoon, Miss Cox. Thank you so much for joining us."

A wave of dread and nausea passed over Bailey as she recognized the man that stood before her. They had been wrong during the entire investigation. Dr. Petrela wasn't the doctor from Revnik after all. And Bailey was more convinced than ever that her fate would be more horrific than she had ever imagined.

TWENTY

The blinking dot disappeared. Frank hit a few buttons on his keyboard, trying to refresh the data, but nothing happened. "We've lost her." He pushed a few more buttons, but still nothing happened.

"How could we have lost her?" Ben asked, glancing over at his partner from time to time as he drove.

"Maybe they discovered the tracker and destroyed it, or maybe they went inside a building or parking deck with tons of concrete."

"Can you pull up the last coordinates that we had?"

"Yeah, that's what I'm doing now." Frank fiddled with the program, trying to fine-tune the location. He knew the device he was using communicated both by GPS and by cell-tower triangulation, and it could usually show him his quarry with startling accuracy. Even so, the device had its limitations, and so did he, even though he'd been trained on how to use the device. He made a few more calculations and found the data he was looking for. "Okay, we lost her somewhere downtown near Bay Street and Newnan Street."

Ben made another turn as Frank called his team and let them know the latest news. They agreed upon a rendezvous at Bailey's last known location. Frank hung up his phone and turned back to Ben. "Okay, what's in that area? There's the Florida Theater and a few office buildings."

"Yeah, and some sort of publishing company. I think there's also a law office or two. That's pretty close to the new courthouse."

Frank was quiet for a moment as the ideas swirled in his head and then he turned on his phone again and called Sergeant Daniels. "Daniels, I need you to run a check on Dr. Petrela, the Balkavian who's the focus of our investigation, and the buildings downtown around Bay and Newnan. See if you can come up with any connections, and call me back as soon as you find something."

He hung up right as he got another notification. Apparently, Bailey's search for the Balkavian doctor had gotten another hit. He was tempted to turn the alert off and look at the image later since he was too worried about Bailey's current predicament to focus on anything else, but something made him wait until the photo loaded. He glanced at the image and then did a double take. There *was* a recognizable face in front of the farmhouse in the picture, but it wasn't the face of Dr. Petrela that Bailey had showed him on her computer when they'd talked about her interview.

It was Dr. David Fredericks, with a white doctor's coat on and a machine gun in his hands.

A sickening feeling swept over him from head to toe. He glanced at Ben, who noticed his change in demeanor.

"What is it?"

"We made a mistake. A big one."

"What are you talking about?"

Frank held up his hand and redialed Sergeant Daniels. "Forget that last request, Sergeant. Instead, do the same search with Dr. David Fredericks instead of Dr. Petrela. I've just gotten new evidence that *he's* our mystery doctor who's guilty of all of those war crimes. He's the one we're after. He has an office in downtown Atlanta. Check his known associates and business interests and see if any of them have any ties to this geographical area, as well. Pull in the FBI and let them know what you're searching for. Got it? And do it all ASAP." He hung up, a grim silence filling the car as Graham continued to drive.

"You know they're going to kill her. Don't you?" Frank asked Ben, a sense of desperation sweeping over him. "They think she knows too much. And now she really does. If they believe that Fredericks's cover is already blown, they'll pump her for what information they can get about how much we know, and then they're going to disappear and relocate. We only have a narrow window to find her."

Ben nodded, agreeing with his friend but either unable or unwilling to make it worse by voicing his own concerns.

"I *have* to find her."

"We'll find her, Frank."

Frank heard his partner's words, but the anxiety wouldn't dissipate. He couldn't bear the thought of Bailey getting hurt. She didn't have to choose him and the relationship he was offering. She just had to survive.

Bailey tried to rise from her chair, but the woman stood behind her and pushed her back down by her shoulder. "So it's you," she said venomously. "Let me guess, you're from a small village named Revnik?"

Fredericks smiled, but it was an evil smile. "Why, yes, I'm flattered that you looked me up. Now I'd like you to tell me the rest of what you know about our little enterprise."

"I'm telling you nothing," she spat. "I can't believe you ordered those men to shoot my father. He was a kind, innocent man. He didn't deserve it."

Fredericks smiled and paced behind his desk. "I've found that people rarely get what they deserve in this life. And, for the record, I barely knew your father. All I can say is that he got in my way. Business comes first in my world. Your father should have stayed away from my concerns."

"Stayed away?" She struggled again to stand, but the woman's grip was fast and strong. "Under penalty of death?"

"I don't take chances, Miss Cox. And of all of the lives you seem to be concerned about, what you should be worrying about right now is your own."

Bailey pressed her lips together. She wanted to blurt out that the sheriff's office and the FBI would soon be breathing down his neck, but she didn't want to give away any information. The sooner he realized how much law enforcement knew about his operation, the sooner he would pull up stakes and disappear. She wanted him caught and punished for his crimes. She had to stay quiet.

Fredericks seemed to be able to read her mind. "Determined to keep your secrets, are you?" He laughed, but there was no mirth in his voice. He opened the drawer to his desk and pulled out a syringe and a small medicine bottle. He drew the medicine into the syringe as he spoke. "I admire your desire to protect your new friends, but, I assure you, you will tell me everything I want to know." He motioned to the driver, who took her crutches and leaned them against the back wall and also grabbed her purse and tossed it into a heap in the corner. Then he returned and joined the woman behind her chair. The next thing she knew, the two of them were holding her down and there was no way to escape.

"What's in the needle?" she asked, squirming. She hated needles to start with, but the idea of some strange medicine flowing through her veins scared her even worse.

"Oh, don't worry," he intoned, again with a sickening smile. "You're young and healthy, which makes you valuable. I wouldn't give you anything that would damage your valuable organs."

"What?" She had guessed his final intentions, but, even so, it was quite sobering to hear her fears voiced out loud. "You're a monster."

He shrugged. "Who's to say? My actions have saved the lives of people all over the world. Is it so bad for me to make some money at the same time?"

"It is when the only people you care about saving are rich people who can afford your services."

"Perhaps."

"And at what cost? What about your innocent victims?"

He shrugged again. "So, you do seem to know a bit about my operation. I was afraid of that." He tied a strip of rubber around her upper arm and turned her wrist over so he could see her veins. "Just relax, my dear. This will all be over very soon." He thumped her vein, apparently satisfied. "You're going to feel a small prick." He injected the needle and pushed the drug into her vein.

Bailey closed her eyes, her mind filled with prayer. God would not leave her or forsake her. Even if this was the end for her, she knew where she was going. She only had one regret—that she would never get a chance to tell Kennedy her true feelings about him. Why had she stayed silent last night? She had fallen in love with Franklin Kennedy but had been too scared to express her emotions. Now she would never get that chance. And what if he never found her? He would think she ran out on him, just like his mother, and that would cause him a great deal of pain. She grimaced, sick with the ramifications of her actions and filled with regret.

She would never go without voicing her feelings again. If God gave her another chance to see Kennedy, she would make sure to tell him how much he meant to her.

Whatever the doctor had given her made her feel warm and relaxed, and she finally stopped fighting and just sat back in the chair. A few moments later, she couldn't even raise her arms, even though she tried, and staying upright in a sitting position took a great deal of effort. She felt her abductor's grips loosen, and a little later they released her completely, apparently knowing that she was no longer a threat.

Fredericks rolled his office chair closer to Bailey, leaned back and crossed his legs. "So tell me, Miss Cox, how much do you know about me?"

"I know you're a murderer," she said softly.

"Yes, we've covered that. Do you know where I'm from?"

"Balkavia," she said softly, unable to stop the words that were pouring from her mouth. Whatever he had given her had completely removed her ability to guard her tongue. "You were a doctor in the BLU. You worked in a farmhouse near Vakamira. You killed hundreds of innocent people and sold their body parts for profit to a doctor in Turkey and probably to others in lots of places. You've been charged in absentia for war crimes."

Fredericks barely reacted to the words she had uttered, but she could see his mouth tighten. She wondered if he practiced that poker face in a mirror. "Go on."

"What else do you want to know?"

"Tell me about my work in the United States. What have I been doing?"

"You have been laundering money from your illegal operations in Europe through a pharmaceutical company in Chicago until recently, when someone discovered what you were doing. You had your team of mercenaries kill all of the men you were working with to cover your tracks. Then you set your sights on becoming CEO of Gates so you could use that company for your illegal operations instead. They're about to get a new contract with Nextco, and I'm thinking you saw that as a golden opportunity to pad the books and launder the cash."

Fredericks's lips thinned even further into a small line, yet he neither confirmed nor denied her words.

"Well? How close am I to the truth?" she challenged. He'd already said he planned to kill her. What difference did it make if she knew the answers to his questions?

"Too close," he said quietly. "You're remarkably well-informed." He stood and brushed at invisible lint on his slacks. "Though you have a total lack of understanding of the history and the politics in Balkavia that led to my work. What I did was necessary. Someone like you would never understand. The conflict in my homeland has been going on for generations. You're a mere baby. How could you possibly comprehend the things I've seen?" He returned to his desk, grabbed a briefcase and walked toward the door. He stopped and moved out of the way as the door opened and the woman pushed a gurney in and put it next to Bailey's chair. Bailey hadn't even realized the woman had left in the first place. She was having trouble keeping up with what was going on around her.

"I can't tell you how much I've enjoyed our little talk, Miss Cox. Unfortunately, it's time for me to go." He gave her a two-finger salute and left, and the next thing she knew, the woman was leaning over her with an evil smile.

"This will all be over soon enough, Cox. Just relax and do as you're told."

As if she could resist when her body had been drugged into submission? She was unable to even lift her arms as the woman and the driver picked her up and put her on the gurney. Then they strapped her down so she would be unable to escape even if she'd had the strength. They wheeled her out and into a service elevator. A few moments later, she was apparently on the roof of the building, and she felt the heat from the sun and the Florida humidity. They had rolled her gurney near a helicopter whose rotors were just starting to turn.

This is it, she thought fleetingly. Once she was on the helicopter, Kennedy would never find either her or Dr. Fredericks. The murderous doctor would escape justice once again and would continue his practice of killing the less fortunate and selling their body parts to the highest bidder. She was sickened at the thought. Dr. Fredericks, the war criminal, had won yet again and she was all set to be his next victim.

TWENTY-ONE

She heard gunfire first, and then bullets seemed to be flying over the entire roof. Both the woman and the driver ducked behind the gurney and tried to return fire, using Bailey as a shield. She watched helplessly as a shot hit the side of the helicopter above her, but she felt no sorrow at all when a bullet hit the woman in the forehead and she fell across Bailey's legs. She didn't know who was firing or why, but anything that slowed her down from being loaded on the helicopter like a piece of luggage was okay with her.

More gunfire erupted, and she felt a bullet hit the gurney above her head. She believed the driver was still back there somewhere, but the drug in her system was so strong that she was unable to even lift her head to look. The driver fired again and again, the gun so loud that her ears began to ring. He fired one last time before a bullet must have caught him because the next thing she heard was his body slump to the ground and his gun clatter on the rooftop. The pilot yelled something about surrendering, and the helicopter's rotors began to slow.

She heard more gunfire, but it only lasted a few more minutes. Then there was nothing but shouting.

"Bailey?"

She couldn't believe her ears. "Kennedy?" How had he found her?

"Bailey, are you okay?"

All of a sudden he was standing above the gurney, and she saw his face and a wave of relief swept over her. "I can't believe you came. How did you find me?"

He checked the Balkavian woman quickly and then pushed her lifeless body off of Bailey's legs and returned to the top of the gurney so she could see him again. "Hold on, Bailey. I'll have you out of there in no time." She could feel him loosening the straps, and a moment later they fell away completely.

He returned once again so she could see him. "Can you stand?"

She shook her head. "No, they gave me something. I don't know what…" Her eyes widened. "It was Fredericks! He was the doctor from Balkavia that killed all of those people. You can't let him escape!"

"It's okay," he said quietly as he leaned closer to her face. "We got him. He was in the helicopter, but he got out to shoot at us when it became clear that the helicopter was hit and couldn't take off. He's dead, Bailey. He'll never hurt anyone again." He kissed her gently on the forehead. "Don't worry. I'm going to take care of you now. You're safe."

Her eyes filled with tears and he wiped them gently away. He leaned closer to her ear and spoke softly for her ears alone. "No, don't cry. I thought I'd lost you, but everything is going to be okay now. I'm going to take you to a hospital. They'll figure out what Fredericks drugged you with and we'll get you back on your feet."

He lifted her carefully into his arms and started carrying her toward the elevator. Bailey smiled, knowing she was right where she needed to be. "I love you, Franklin Kennedy."

He paused and met her eyes, and she saw nothing but warmth and caring reflected back at her. "I love you back, Bailey."

Frank paced, waiting for the doctor to finish with Bailey. It had been several hours since they'd first arrived, and Bailey's condition had already drastically improved, but she had been sleeping most of that time and they still hadn't had an opportunity to talk.

She loved him. Could those words she had uttered in her drugged condition actually be true? He dared to hope but, at the same time, was afraid that she had said them only because she'd thought she was about to die.

Ben walked up to his side and gave him the update from the crime scene. Frank noticed the weariness in his eyes but also the elation that came from a successful conclusion. David Fredericks was dead. He would never hurt anyone ever again. He motioned toward Bailey's purse that Ben had clutched in his hand.

"That's not your color."

Ben laughed. "This is Bailey's. I thought you'd want to give it back to her." He held it out and Frank took it, along with the crutches she had been using. Frank wanted to ask Ben about the contents of the purse but was afraid of the answer. He was pretty sure the fake passport he'd seen Bailey purchase in the surveillance video was still inside.

Ben seemed to anticipate his question. "I think you're gonna want to see something in there, but maybe Bailey should be the one to give it to you."

Frank raised an eyebrow at Ben's riddle. "What does that mean?"

"Just trust me."

"Okay."

"Has the boss called you?" Ben asked.

"Yeah. He's developed a good plan for Bailey. I haven't had a chance to talk to her, though. I'll let her know her options once she wakes up and the doctor lets me go in there. I don't know what she's going to do. The ball's in her court now."

Ben smiled, a knowing look on his face.

Frank good-naturedly punched him in the arm. "What?"

The doctor came out and approached the men before Ben could answer, and Frank was happy for the interruption. The doctor made a few more notes on his tablet and then turned his attention to them. "Hello, gentlemen."

"How's our patient doing?" Frank asked.

"Much better," the doctor answered. "The worst of the drug has worn off now and I think she's feeling more like her old self. After another couple hours of observation, she'll be able to go home. She's awake and you can see her if you want to."

Frank smiled. "That's great to hear. Thanks for taking such good care of her."

The doctor shook his head. "I haven't done much. That lady is a fighter. I don't think anything could hold her down for very long."

Ben nodded. "You could say that again." He turned to his friend and watched as the doctor walked away. "Okay, Frankie. I'm headed out. Call me if you need me."

"Deal."

Frank said a small prayer of thankfulness and paused a moment with his hand on the door. He was in a hurry to see her, and yet, at the same time, he was afraid that despite her words of love, she would still want to run if given the chance.

What would Bailey choose?

He opened the door slowly and she didn't notice him at first. He leaned the crutches against the wall by the door and the movement caught her eye.

"Hi," Frank said softly.

"Hi, yourself."

"Ben Graham found your purse and crutches and brought them over." He put her purse on the table by her bed.

She nodded. "I'll have to remember to thank him."

"How do you feel?"

"Just tired, mostly. My memory is a bit hazy about what happened. I remember Fredericks giving me some sort of injection, and after that I just recall bits and pieces."

Frank wasn't expecting that. He wondered if she even remembered her profession of love. He tried to convince himself that it didn't matter, but he was unsuccessful. He pulled up a chair and sat down near her bed. He didn't want her to feel threatened in any way by his presence, and even though she was smiling, he was still unsure of her intentions. Would she stay? Would she tell him she loved him again?

She turned her head and met his eyes. "So is it over? I do remember you telling me Fredericks is dead."

"Yes, that's right. The FBI is taking over the bulk of the case now since it has multi-state implications. We'll be helping out here and there, but they'll be running point. They believe, and I agree, that with Fredericks dead, the threat against us is over. They'll continue working with Interpol to tie up the rest of the loose ends."

She raised an eyebrow at his long-winded response and he mentally kicked himself for letting his insecurity get the best of him. He never rambled unless he was nervous. He couldn't remember the last time he had felt as nervous as he did right now. "Your quest for justice is finished, Bailey. Your father's death has been avenged."

She leaned back a bit, absorbing his words. "The world is a better place without Fredericks in it."

"Agreed. In fact, every Balkavian on that rooftop who was part of his team is dead too, except the helicopter pilot, who surrendered. Turns out he was just a local boy who had been hired to fly, so he wasn't really one of them. He seemed pretty shocked when we told him what they were involved in."

"Wow." She seemed to let that soak in. "What about Gates? Were they involved in the money laundering?"

Frank shook his head. "It doesn't look that way, but the forensic accounting team is still taking a hard look at their books. But since Fredericks hadn't actually started working there yet, he hadn't had the chance to do any damage, so we're not expecting to uncover anything out of place. So far, everything we're finding there is legit, and the board and leadership were all appalled at what almost happened. According to Mr. Johnson, it looks like Clarissa Merritt, the pediatric oncologist, will probably end up with the job."

"So Fredericks was willing to kill anyone who got in his way of becoming CEO?"

"Yes. Now that the Balkavians have run out of ways to hide the money in the US, Interpol and the FBI are hoping to be able to track down the rest of the operation in Europe. They'll keep us informed of their progress."

Bailey was silent for a minute as she seemed to be absorbing all of the new information. "So what about Dr. Petrela? What's his story?"

"Apparently, he was a soldier and paramedic with the BLU, and his connections and experience from that stint helped him get the falsified documents he needed to fake his medical degree. However, he wasn't involved in anything criminal related to Dr. Fredericks, or the Farmhouse crimes. We still haven't found him, but there has been a warrant issued for his arrest for practicing medicine without a license. I doubt we'll ever find him, though. My guess is, he returned to Balkavia with his family."

There was silence in the room for a moment, and Bailey wondered what was keeping Kennedy from snapping on the cuffs. Maybe he figured that there was no need to rush since she wouldn't be able to escape him.

But the doctor had already explained to her that she would be released in an hour or so, so Kennedy's presence must mean that he was here to transport her to jail once the doctor was done with her. He had her purse, so he must have seen the contents. It was odd that he hadn't mentioned anything about the passport. She thought she might as well ask and clear the air.

"So, what are you going to do with the gift I gave you?"

Kennedy leaned forward, his expression one of confusion. "What gift?"

She motioned toward her purse. "Didn't you get it yet? I figured you must have found it already."

"I don't know what you're talking about."

Bailey pulled herself to a sitting position and reached over to grab her purse. She opened it and pulled out the manila envelope. The seal had been broken. "I don't know who opened it, but this envelope is for you."

He took the packet and stopped when he noticed that it had been addressed to him. He opened it and saw the fake passport and IDs, as well as the note she'd written giving him the documents. "You don't look like a Melissa."

She laughed. "I know, right? I told my friend that too." She balled the sheet up in her hand, nervousness overwhelming her. Was she making the right decision? She looked into his green eyes and could see the answer. Yes. This time she was finally doing the right thing.

"I ordered these a while ago, so I had to go through with the purchase, but I don't need them now. I've decided to stay and go back to jail and face the consequences of my actions. That's why I'm giving these to you, so I'm not tempted to use them if the going gets tough."

She bit her bottom lip, unsure how he would react, but the next thing she knew he had stood, moved to her side in the bed and pulled her into a warm embrace. "I'm so glad you made the right decision. I saw the sale on the surveillance video when we were trying to figure out what had happened to you, and I'd feared the worst."

She felt so safe, so cherished in his arms. She couldn't remember ever feeling so loved. She wasn't sure she'd told him her feelings yet, and it was definitely time to do so. "I love you, Franklin Kennedy. I know you may not want to wait for me like you promised, but I want to thank you for believing in me and helping me make the right choices."

He pulled back a bit and she could see his eyes. "Of course I'm sticking by you and keeping my promise. You mean the world to me." He leaned forward and kissed her gently. "You should also know that my boss has an idea that you might like. He wants to know if you'll come to work for the sheriff's office in our IT department. We need a good computer expert to help us with our detective work."

"But I thought I was going to jail?"

Kennedy gently touched her lips with his thumb, effectively silencing her. "Well, before you decide, listen to his offer. If you take the job, there are a few conditions. First of all, it would be part of a plea bargain. You'd still have to plead *nolo contendere* to the felony charge."

"What's the rest of the deal?"

Kennedy smiled. "You have to agree to work with

us for four years and will remain on probation during that time, as well. You'll also have to do one hundred community service hours in addition to your work for us. The job is only entry-level, and the pay isn't great, but you'll be assigned to my division in our IT department so I can keep an eye on you."

She laughed in joy and he leaned forward and their lips met. The kiss was tentative at first, but then nothing was held back and Bailey wrapped her arms around him. Finally, she broke off the kiss so she could say what was on her heart.

"I love you, Franklin Kennedy."

She knew she would never get tired of saying those words, and from Kennedy's expression, she doubted he would ever get tired of hearing them. His smile was ear to ear.

"I love you back, Bailey."

* * * * *

If you loved this book, don't miss these
other action-packed Kathleen Tailer stories:

UNDER THE MARSHAL'S PROTECTION
THE RELUCTANT WITNESS
PERILOUS REFUGE

Find more great reads at www.LoveInspired.com.

Dear Reader,

Although this book is a work of fiction, many of my ideas came from researching the pain and suffering that occurred in Albania in 1999. War is horrific, and oftentimes has unintended consequences.

The characters in this book are flawed, just like the rest of us, but, with God's help, they manage to grow during their trials. My hope is that this book will encourage you to see the beauty around you and remember that God is always with you; He will never leave you or forsake you, no matter what the circumstances.

Thank you for sharing your time with me!

Kathleen Tailer

Get 2 Free Books,
Plus 2 Free Gifts—
just for trying the Reader Service!